KNOW YOU MORE

BOOKS BY JAN THOMPSON

CITY/COASTAL/BEACH ROMANCE

Seaside Chapel (7 Books)

JanThompson.com/seaside

Savannah Sweethearts (12 Books)

JanThompson.com/savannah

Vacation Sweethearts (8 Books)

JanThompson.com/vacation

ROMANTIC SUSPENSE/THRILLERS

Protector Sweethearts (6 Books)

JanThompson.com/protector

Defender Sweethearts (6 Books)

JanThompson.com/defender

Binary Hackers (4 Books)

JanThompson.com/binary

JanThompson.com/books

KNOW YOU MORE

SAVANNAH SWEETHEARTS
BOOK TWO

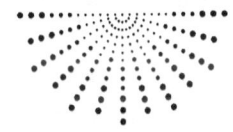

JAN THOMPSON

GEORGIA
PRESS

KNOW YOU MORE (SAVANNAH
SWEETHEARTS BOOK 2)

Copyright © 2015 Jan Edttii Lim Thompson

Book News: JanThompson.com/newsletter
Author Website: JanThompson.com
Published by Georgia Press LLC

This book is a work of fiction. All characters, persons, places,
events, and things either are the product of the author's active
imagination or are used fictitiously.

Scripture taken from the New King James Version®. Copyright
© 1982 by Thomas Nelson. Used by permission. All rights
reserved.

eBook Cover Design: Georgia Press LLC
Paperback Cover Design: Georgia Press and Deranged Doctor
Design

eBook ISBN 978-1-944188-01-6
Paperback ISBN 978-1-944188-25-2

To my Lord and Savior, Jesus Christ, who died on the cross to save me from my sins and rose again from the grave to give me eternal life in heaven.

～

For God so loved the world that He gave His only begotten Son, that whoever believes in Him should not perish but have everlasting life.
—John 3:16

READ A FREE EBOOK IN THE SAME STORY WORLD

Set in Georgia, South Carolina, and Tennessee, this clean and wholesome Christian romance tells the story of art gallery archivist Sheryl Breckenridge and world-famous sculptor Winton Pace. Read this ebook for free!

Time for Me (A Vacation Sweethearts Prequel)
JanThompson.com/time-free

YOU ARE READING KNOW YOU MORE

SAVANNAH SWEETHEARTS BOOK 2

He loves her...
He loves her not...
She's waiting for him to decide.

A young pastor of a growing church in a thriving community, Diego Flores has to come to grips with God's will for his church and his personal life.

A Christian beach romance featuring life in a small church, *Know You More* is Book 2 in *USA Today* bestselling author Jan Thompson's Savannah Sweethearts series of clean and wholesome, sweet and inspirational, contemporary Christian romances set in the coastal city of Savannah, Georgia, and on the beaches of Tybee Island by the Atlantic Ocean.

DIEGO'S DISQUIET...

Diego Flores has been interested in his best friend's younger sister since their college days, but his calling to grow Riverside Chapel takes up most of his time.

When Heidi Wei becomes his strongest supporter in his church-planting ministry, how does Diego show his feelings for her without giving her the wrong idea?

Does she see him as potential husband material or just the pastor of their church?

HEIDI'S HURDLES...

Heidi suspects that Diego is sweet on her, but he seems to believe that his divine calling prevents him from acting on it. If it isn't meant to be, she's not going to push for it.

Yet every time they are together, something happens between them. Have they moved beyond the platonic relationship they have enjoyed all these years to something more personal?

When a crisis hits Heidi's family, Diego has to balance pastoring his congregation and ministering to Heidi without losing either one. Being in love while growing a new church is difficult for him to juggle. Which path is more important? Which one should he focus on?

Know You More (Savannah Sweethearts Book 2):
JanThompson.com/know

Savannah Sweethearts:
JanThompson.com/sweethearts

For book news, sign up for Jan's mailing list:
JanThompson.com/newsletter

KNOW YOU MORE

CHAPTER ONE

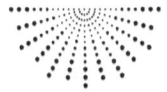

"You can't be in grad school forever." Aidan Ming Wei flipped the salmon burger on his Weber grill. He left the cover open.

On the other side of the grill, the chain-link fence stretched from bushes to sea oat dunes and then wrapped around the side yard of the old beach house.

"Why not?" Heidi couldn't believe her brother brought it up. Again. They'd been through this numerous times. Each time they'd ended up at an impasse.

"At some point in time, you'll need to get out there in the working world—the real world—and get a full-time job."

Heidi felt hurt at Ming's words. "Are you trying to get rid of me?"

"No—"

"Look, I offered to pay rent—"

"Not that." Ming reached for the platter in Heidi's hand. "I'm just wondering how many doctorates you need before any museum would hire you. You have one. Isn't that enough?"

Heidi said nothing. The aroma of salmon calmed her mien, and she was salivating at their dinner. Ming had always done that for her, cooking her favorite meals, taking her to her favorite places. She'd tried not to use the word *favorite* whenever she told him things, or he'd sacrifice for her.

There was no need, really.

She loved him regardless of what he did or didn't do for her. Ever since their parents died—

She sniffed.

Ming stiffened. "Let's talk about this later."

"No. Let's talk about this now and get it over with. What do you really want to say to me, Aidan Ming Wei?" She only called him by his full name when she was mad at him. That was getting increasingly rare since their parents had passed away. It had been seven years. "We've always been honest with each other. Out with it. I can handle it."

"After dinner."

"Now. You started it." Heidi followed her

brother through the back porch, past his old hammock, and into the kitchen-cum-dining room.

"Okay." Ming set the platter on the table.

Heidi had set the table earlier. She sat down adjacent to him.

"Even the president of UGA doesn't have two PhDs," Ming said. "In history, no less."

"Meaning what?"

"Meaning there comes a point in time when school is over, you graduate, and you move on in life."

"I like being on campus."

"Then teach. You'll still be on campus."

"It's not about the money."

"Did I say it was?" Ming looked hurt. "I guess I'm thinking aloud, Heidi. We're in our twenties, but I'd hate to see us exactly as we are fifty years from now."

"But I love salmon. That can stay the same," Heidi joked. "Seriously, it's hard to have something different when..."

Heidi went silent and Ming didn't pry.

"I miss them so much," Heidi said.

"Me too." Ming reached for her. They held hands for a while. "But if you asked them, they wouldn't want to come back here. Heaven is perfect, and they're having a great time. We just have to trust God to take care of us down here until we see them again. All right?"

Heidi nodded. The tears flowed nonetheless.

"Heidi." Ming's voice seemed broken, defeated. "I'm sorry I brought any of it up. I ruined our dinner."

"No. You cooked me salmon. You made my day."

"You're so positive and I'm so negative."

"What are siblings for?" Heidi laughed. "You're right, you know. I need to be done with school."

"For the second time, Dr. Wei. Two PhDs. For what? Seems like a waste of time."

"Ha-ha. We'll talk later. Let's eat. Say grace."

Ming chuckled. "Diego was right."

"Diego? How did he get into this conversation?"

"He told me the other day—never mind."

"What did he say?"

"Uh, I said it first, so technically it's not his fault."

"Said what first?"

"You're bossy."

Heidi's eyes flared. "And he agreed?"

"For the record, he calls me bossy too." Before Heidi could reply to that, Ming bowed his head and began praying.

Heidi let it go.

When Ming finished, they ate in silence.

"I'm sorry," Heidi said when they cleared their dinner plates.

"For what?"

"For using up all my money to get these useless degrees."

Ming placed a warm hand on her shoulder. "Come to think of it, doctorates are not entirely useless. They're pretty good academic exercises."

"You were right, you know. What am I going to use them for?"

"You could always teach. Runs in the family, after all."

Yeah. Runs in the family.

Their parents had both been academic. Their research had taken them far and wide to study languages, cultures, and peoples. It was tragic that they had perished in that plane crash on their last short-term mission trip to the South Pacific. Their bodies had never been recovered.

Lost at sea and nothing left of them to bury.

Heidi watched her brother go for the apple pie they'd bought from the grocery store.

"Want some?" His piece was huge.

"No, thanks. I had some earlier this afternoon."

"That's why half of this is gone."

Heidi elbowed him on the way to the sink. She wrung out a damp dishcloth to wipe down their glass dinner table. They'd had that table for a couple of years. It seemed misplaced and mismatched, but neither she nor Ming cared. Much of their furniture was from their parents' old house in Jacksonville. The rest of the items were from donations, consignment sales, thrift shops, wherever they could find solid furniture they could use.

We.

But not really.

This house was not Heidi's. She had owned a townhouse once, but she had been so lonely there that she had sold it and used the money to pay for graduate school. Pretty soon she'd be running out of money if she didn't do something with her degrees.

Her brother was right.

You can't be in grad school forever.

CHAPTER TWO

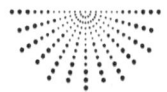

*D*iego Flores stepped onto the small landing inside the front door. He wondered how Ming could live in such cramped quarters.

"The hospital rounds took longer than I'd expected." Diego looked around. He didn't see anyone else besides Ming. "Sorry I'm half an hour late to my own meeting."

"Late? We're never late for desserts." Ming took the container of cupcakes away from Diego. "You made these?"

"As requested. Where's everybody?"

"You know Nadine can't make it. Has to work. That girl doesn't sleep."

"Yeah. She texted me."

"Neither can Simon. He texted me. And

Abilene is still in New Orleans visiting family." Ming stuffed a cupcake into his mouth. He could barely talk. It came out muffled. "Cam and Roger will be late."

Or something that sounded like that. Diego shook his head. "I call for a committee meeting, and half the people don't show up, and most of them didn't bother to let me know."

"Hey, we're a small church." Ming handed Diego a cupcake and a paper napkin. "What did you expect? A hundred people at this meeting? That's even more than the church membership."

"Don't remind me. Riverside Chapel is eighteen months old, and all we have are thirty-some members." Diego plopped down onto a leather armchair just as his iPhone pinged. He checked it. Another church member needing prayer. No rest for the pastor.

"Tell me it's not Mrs. Untermeyer again," Ming said.

"You wish. Next time she calls, I'll forward her to your phone."

"Ha-ha." Ming sat down on a ratty old couch. His cupcake was down to crumbs.

Diego found it interesting that apparently Ming couldn't tell the difference in the ingredients. Diego hadn't put any sugar in the batter, only honey. Ming ate anything. Ever since their college days, whatever

Diego didn't care to eat, he could always feed it to Ming.

Diego ate his cupcake slowly. Not bad, if he didn't say so himself.

He'd been nervous making the cupcakes, packing them, and driving them here. He was always nervous when he came over to Ming's house. He should ask God to calm him, but he felt that his prayers had been ineffective lately. So would God answer this special prayer he prayed every time he parked outside Ming's front door?

The other prayers seemed too easy compared to this.

For one, he had prayed for an increase in church membership. He had even given God the time frame and all. And yet, God had chosen to delay the growth. Obviously, God knew that if the church didn't show a trajectory of growth, he could lose funding from all those faith-promise mission funds at various churches he was affiliated with in the southern USA. They'd all want to see a return in their investments. His modest goal of fifty people by Christmas had been acceptable to his donors.

That was one thing.

This other thing...

Here. Tonight. Now.

He had to dislodge his heart from his throat every time he saw Heidi. Heidi with the wavy hair that swirled with the ocean winds. Heidi with the big brown eyes that saw through his heart and soul, and lips that asked to be—

He blinked.

Speaking of Heidi, where is she?

"Oh, she's in her room," Ming said.

Whoa. Had he spoken those words aloud? What else had he spoken aloud? "I was just wondering."

Ming grinned. "You've been wondering about my sister since UGA."

Diego didn't reply. Yes, it had been years since they were at the University of Georgia.

"Did someone say UGA?" It was Heidi's voice.

Neither Diego nor Ming said a word.

As Heidi came down the hallway, Diego could envision her in a wed—

"Hey." Heidi floated toward him but made an abrupt turn for a side table. "Ooh, cupcakes. Who made these?"

Ming pointed to Diego.

"Let's see." She took a bite. Closed her eyes. "Mmmm."

"Are you staying for the meeting tonight?" Diego's voice was raspy all of a sudden.

"Only for part of it. Have some research to do." Heidi finished the cupcake. Took another one.

"I'm glad you like it." It was all Diego could say.

10

"Like it? Love it!" She wiped her lips. "Where's Cam?"

Why is she asking about Camden? Handsome, cute, eligible Camden?

Diego was surprised at his thoughts. He'd never pegged himself as being a jealous guy or anything like that.

"Cam will be late," Ming answered when nobody else said anything.

Diego settled on a couch across from Ming. "I guess we can get the meeting started. Latecomers can read the minutes later."

Heidi sat down next to Diego and leaned over to look at his iPad. "Ah, just as I'd suspected."

"Suspected?" Diego's palms began to sweat.

"Do you ever do anything without a checklist?" Heidi asked.

Diego had to think about that a bit. And then he thought some more. "No, I don't suppose so."

"What I thought."

"What do you mean?"

"Nothing." Heidi simply smiled.

"It saves time when you make a list."

"No need to defend yourself." Heidi leaned back where she sat.

Diego was surprised she wasn't going to sit somewhere else. There was plenty of room in the living room, considering there were only three people there at the moment. He didn't realize he was staring at her until Heidi nudged him.

"Pray so we can start the meeting, Diego."

"Yes, ma'am." She smelled fresh. Soap fresh, shower fresh. Diego cleared his throat. "I do have some exciting news, but it depends on how we look at it."

CHAPTER THREE

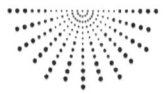

"*A* what?" Ming laughed so hard Heidi thought Mom's china cabinet behind the couch he was reclining on was going to rattle and all the old finds would tumble out. "Is this a joke?"

"No, sir," Diego said. "It's a real riverboat, one of the two currently docked at the waterfront."

To Heidi, Diego seemed unperturbed by Ming's reaction to the news.

"What do y'all think about holding services on a riverboat?" Diego continued.

"Did you just say y'all?" Ming stared in disbelief. "You turning southern now?"

"Working on it."

"You'll never be native, Diego." Ming wiped tears from his eyes. "You need to say it like 'yawl,' you know. Rhymes with 'shawl.'"

"Does not."

"Does too."

Heidi watched the two men. "Boys."

"Just trying to teach this southern Californian some southern Georgian, sis."

They kept on.

"Boys!" Heidi put her hand on Diego's arm. It was right there. And oh boy, it was firm.

Diego stopped talking, his eyes on her hand.

Feeling self-conscious, Heidi pulled back her hand. "I have assignments to complete tonight, so I'm gone in half an hour whether we finish this meeting or not. So. What's the rent, Diego?"

"Free." Diego's voice was quiet. Then it rose again. "We only pay utilities. Jerome said as long as we clean up the place after services, we can use it."

"For how long?" Heidi asked. Across the coffee table, Ming was choking on a cupcake.

"For two years."

"When he said we do the cleaning, did he mean housekeeping? Like doing the windows and cleaning the toilets?"

"Yes. Do you think we're up to it?" Diego looked at Heidi, then at Ming, and then back to Heidi.

"If we work together, yes. You've always said you want to run this church debt-free."

"You were listening."

"I always listen to you, Diego." Heidi was being honest.

"You do?"

Heidi ignored that. She leaned toward his iPad again. "What's the next item on your agenda?"

"Before we get to the next thing, let's wrap up item number one. We can't take a vote on the riverboat offer because we don't have a majority."

"You're the pastor, Diego. Aren't you majority enough?"

"Yes, the buck stops with me as I prayerfully make the final decision, but I want to hear from everyone in my advisory council."

"Truly, Diego, God is the only Adviser you need."

Diego just stared at her.

"What does God say about the riverboat?" Heidi went on.

"We've prayed for the last six months for a new place to meet. The storefront rent is unsustainable, and our lease is up. Our supporting churches have been asking us how many new members we've added, and they don't like the slow growth."

"Missions committees in churches used to be more patient with church planting."

"It's the economic times."

"And the sign of the times," Heidi added.

"To tell you the truth, friends, it's hard growing a church," Diego confessed.

Heidi smiled. "It's God's church. You plant. Someone else waters. He grows. Remember? We even call it church planting, for some reason."

"Wow, Heidi."

"What?"

"I love the way you think. I mean, *like*! I like the way you think."

Heidi shrugged. "Bottom line, do you think God has provided a free place for Riverside Chapel to hold church services?"

"I was expecting a building on land," Diego said.

"How many people can the riverboat seat?"

"It has two dining rooms. Each can hold two hundred people."

"Since we have fewer than forty people right now, there's room to grow, right?"

"I agree. But we might have to do live feeds to the second room if we max out at two hundred."

"That's a nice number of members to have." Heidi felt annoyed that her brother was on his iPhone again. She frowned.

Ming lifted his index finger. "One sec."

Heidi turned back to Diego. "When God provides in unexpected ways, I would be grateful."

"For the riverboat, you mean?"

"For anything, Diego. Whatever we have—the little, the much—all come from God."

When Diego said nothing to her statement, Heidi felt uncomfortable. "Don't listen to me. You went to seminary. I did not. I have no idea what I'm talking about. And I certainly don't put any of it into practice."

"I'm listening, Heidi. You think the riverboat is a gift from God."

Heidi nodded. "We prayed for a place to meet that's better than the shop at the corner of expensive and invisible. Here it is. Front and center, parked at the most touristy place of all Savannah. And free."

"They don't *park* riverboats, Heidi." Ming joined the conversation.

"Whatever."

Diego leaned forward, his iPad still in hand. "Kind of a strange venue, don't you think?"

"Not really." Heidi got up to get more cupcakes. She passed the tray around. "Jesus preached from a boat, remember?"

Diego nodded.

"He stood on a boat and preached to the people standing on shore." Heidi knew Diego didn't need her to remind him of the Bible passage.

Ming reached for another cupcake from the tray that Heidi had set down. "Heidi has a point. I say go for it, Diego. If we keep our costs down, we could do more ministry work."

"I agree," Heidi said.

"And yet?" Diego asked.

"I know you don't make quick decisions," she said.

"I try to be careful."

"Too careful."

"You think so?"

Heidi chuckled. "Yes. You said at my college commencement party at UGA that God had called you to plant a church. Five years later you were still an assistant pastor at Midtown Chapel. Remember that?"

"Well, God's timing can't be rushed," Diego said.

"Yes, but if He has timed it, don't miss the window."

Diego looked at her kind of oddly. "You think this riverboat is a divine window."

"Yes, I do. It's in a high-visibility area. What about permits to hold a church service and all?"

"We'll sort that out. Shouldn't be too hard to get. After all, Jerome already holds Christian weddings there. I officiated one last spring. That's how we got to talking, really."

"And that was how Jerome got saved." Heidi's

eyes brightened. "See how God has provided? He worked out all things for our good."

"Wow, Heidi."

"That's the second time you said that tonight." Heidi glanced at the clock on the wall, but she didn't move. She could do her assignments later. This was more important. Diego needed help.

Help?

Sigh.

Who was she to advise the pastor of her church? She couldn't even get her own life together. Somehow, strangely enough, she saw how God had provided for Riverside Chapel. It was as clear as day. If only Diego saw it too.

Diego turned his head. "I know you have to go."

"I'll stay a bit longer."

"What about your homework?"

"I'll do it tomorrow. It's not due until next week anyway." She had hoped to finish her assignments early, but this was more important. Diego needed their input so he could make the right decision for Riverside Chapel.

"I appreciate what you said about the riverboat," Diego said. "I've been praying about it."

"Don't take too long." Heidi didn't think her voice was loud enough for Ming to hear.

Across the table, Ming lost it. "You're one to

talk, sis. Look how long it takes you to decide on your career."

"I'm working on it." Heidi glanced at Diego. "He's trying to embarrass me in front of you again."

Ming laughed. "Diego knows all about us, and yet he still hangs out with us."

"Thanks, guys. Tell you what. I'll pray about this a bit more and let you know," Diego said. "Does that sound good?"

"Perfect," Heidi said. "What's next on the agenda?"

"Our ministry to shut-ins."

Ming groaned. "I'm afraid I'll have to bail out of that again."

"We don't have enough church members to rotate visiting shut-ins."

"I hear you, Diego. I'm trying to keep my business afloat."

Heidi tried to read her brother's face, but he didn't show what he was feeling. Still, she had heard some of his conversations of late, how the clients had thinned out at Savannah River Investigations. He had to let his office manager go. If he didn't get new contracts soon, the private investigation firm would close.

And Ming would lose this beach house.

Heidi had better get a job soon to help out. She remembered those job listings she'd seen on the campus website. One of them was a research position in Milledgeville, digging around the Confederate Andersonville Prison. She could apply for that job using her first PhD alone. Her dissertation had been on the Civil War, after all.

"We can't just send anyone to see the senior citizens," Diego said. "I prefer church members of some standing."

"That way they can represent Riverside Chapel well," Heidi added.

"Right. I'd rather not send new members before they complete the new members' class. Some of them are newly saved. I would prefer more seasoned believers. Right now, Roger, Nadine, Abilene, and I are doing all the visits. I'm surprised at the number of invalid senior adults living in coastal Georgia."

"We can't visit everyone." Ming folded his arms across his chest.

Some kind of silence swept through the living room.

Heidi couldn't bear it. "I'll go, Diego."

Diego smiled. It was that happy smile she'd seen before when he was at ease.

But she didn't volunteer to make him happy. She volunteered because there was a need in the ministry and she could fill it. She hadn't seen the need before, but people's schedules changed.

If God wanted her to visit these elderly friends

or soon-to-be friends, He would somehow fit it into her busy schedule. That would ease up Ming's tension, and he wouldn't feel forced to volunteer. She didn't want him to have any more pressure past his job. If she could alleviate that pressure, then maybe Ming wouldn't miss church services as much as he had the last several months he had been doing some undercover work for the Feds.

"I'll go—oh, but I don't have a reliable car." *Oh dear. What have I signed up for?*

"Don't worry about that." Diego patted Heidi's shoulder. "I'll pick you up."

CHAPTER FOUR

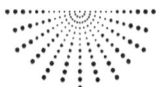

I can't believe I suggested carpooling!

Diego groaned as he backed his car out of Ming's driveway and joined the traffic going toward his apartment in downtown Savannah.

"I can't be in the same car as Heidi, Lord." Diego shook his head. He waited to hear if God would say something to him.

This was his praying car, as he called it. Whenever he drove in this car alone, he would pray aloud. Sure, God could hear him even if he prayed in silence. In fact, God could hear his heart before he said a word of prayer. Yet voicing his prayer aloud helped clarify his thinking.

Uh, maybe.

He glanced around to make sure he had rolled up the windows. No point looking like a fool to other drivers zipping around him. His lamentations were only between him and his God.

What if this is the Lord's doing?

"But I can't think of Heidi. I need to focus on growing Riverside. Thirty members do not a church make."

Then the words in the New Testament came back to his mind. A verse he had memorized a long time ago in high school. Matthew 18:20.

He recited it aloud.

For where two or three are gathered together in My name, I am there in the midst of them.

God had already begun the church.

He shouldn't be complaining at all. Thirty-some people was a small church, but it was a church nonetheless, though it had taken them eighteen months to get this far.

What Heidi had said at that evening's meeting came to his mind.

It's God's church. You plant. Someone else waters. He grows. Remember? We even call it church planting, for some reason.

Diego recalled all the times Heidi had been an encourager to him. As far back as when the three of them had been at the University of Georgia, those days before Diego had felt the call to pastoral ministry and transferred out to a Bible college.

He remembered when he flunked college physics. Heidi had baked some cookies to cheer him up. They were missing a few ingredients, like sugar. The blobs-of-whatever were stuck to the cookie sheet, and had burnt so badly that they had to open all the windows to Ming's smoky apartment.

Helpful Heidi.

If Diego could ever afford a ministry assistant, Heidi would be his first candidate. It would be helpful to the entire ministry to have her alongside him. He listened to her, trusted her, and valued her. She wouldn't undermine his leadership. She would tell him the truth about everything, even if it hurt.

Like that time he had broken up with his girl-friend who didn't want to be a missionary. She hadn't understood that from time to time, Diego felt the calling to be a missionary to Mongolia. Not even to modern Ulan Bator, but to the hinterlands of the back side of unknown mountains where there was no running water or electricity.

Yep. Right in the middle of nowhere where nobody lived.

Exactly.

Where nobody lived.

Heidi, on the other hand, had pointed out that if God had called Diego there, then there would be at least one person waiting at that location for him to witness to.

Wow, Heidi.

After much prayer, Diego had no longer felt the need to go. Perhaps nationals would do better reaching their own people rather than a stranger from Irvine. He had no language or survival skills and no supporting mission board. He couldn't imagine dragging a reluctant bride across twelve time zones to a place in the middle of nowhere to witness to one yak herder.

It would take a special pastor's wife to go with him to the edge of the world, Heidi had said.

A special pastor's wife.

There was only one person Diego could think of. He smiled as he stopped at a red light. "She'd enjoy every moment of it. And she'd probably write books about the history of yak herding, although, yeah, she herself needs some counseling regarding her own stagnant career."

Diego had much counsel to offer her on her career, and in turn, she had some great ideas for his leading Riverside Chapel.

"We sure could work well together." He turned his blinker on. He didn't know how he made it here into downtown Savannah this soon. He hoped he hadn't been speeding, but he hadn't paid attention to the speedometer. All he had in his mind was—

That's bad.

"Forgive me, Lord. I can't be thinking of Heidi. I need to be thinking of Riverside Chapel. You've given me a job. I'm getting more and more distracted. My flesh is weak. I think I'm in love. I've been in love for five years. But I can't be. Not now. Not when I need to plant this church!"

What in the world was all that mumbo jumbo that had just come out of his mouth?

Diego decided he needed to spend more time praying and studying God's word. He had been trying to memorize the book of Ephesians. It was time to step it up and speed it up.

Yeah. That'd take his mind off Heidi Wei, the one he couldn't possibly have.

"Lord, teach me to be content as a single man." As soon as he spoke it, Diego knew he didn't want God to give him what he asked.

CHAPTER FIVE

*H*eidi Wei ate her chicken salad lunch in the September sunshine while waiting for Ming to pick her up. They had agreed to meet at this bench outside the Oglethorpe Building at the University of Coastal Georgia. It was one building over from the Department of History, where most of her fellow graduate students were studying for obscure degrees and writing dissertations that maybe five people in all the world, at most, would read.

Dissertations like "The Generational Economic Repercussions of the Indentured Servitudes of Young Unmarried European Women in the Early Days of the British Colonies of Savannah, Fort Frederica, Darien, and Ebenezer on Modern Georgia in the Twenty-First Century."

Well, at least I picked a descriptive title.

On the one hand, all the historical facts were there. She had a perpetual membership at the Georgia Historical Society's vast library of first-person accounts. She'd read the Trustee letters and personal journals countless times. She could feel the pulse of General James Oglethorpe, who'd founded Savannah, and thus, Georgia, and William Stephens, the secretary and president of England's thirteenth and last colony in America.

That was Georgia's history in those handwritten documents, carefully preserved in temperature-controlled vaults both here in Savannah and at the Hargrett Rare Book & Manuscript Library at the University of Georgia.

All she had to do was read and write.

Heidi threw out her lunch container in a recycling bin and sat back down on the bench.

Where in the world is Ming?

She texted him again.

No response.

Maybe he had forgotten to recharge his iPhone. He did that sometimes.

Heidi was retrieving her laptop from her backpack when she spotted a charcoal-colored Toyota pulling up to the curb.

Uh-oh. Diego.

He rolled down his window and waved.

Heidi smiled, put away her laptop, and walked toward Diego. "Where's my brother?"

"He's delayed. I'm giving you a ride home."

"It's out of your way." Heidi stood outside the car. "It's a good half an hour from here to Tybee without traffic."

"I don't mind. Get in."

So Heidi did. She hugged her backpack on her lap.

"Why don't we put the backpack in the back?" Diego suggested.

"Okay."

With one arm, he hoisted the backpack between the seats and gently put it down on the floor behind them. "What do you have in here? Bricks?"

"Books."

"Don't they have ebooks?"

"They're very old books."

"The publishers could've made ebook editions."

"Yeah, but there's nothing like holding paper in your hand, you know."

"Ah. I forget you're a historian."

"I will be once I finish." Again.

"When does your dissertation go before the board?"

"End of this semester. Then I'm done."

"Done with school?"

"Yeah. Ming says I need to get out into the *real*

world and get a *real* job. Apparently being a student doesn't count."

"We're all students in this life."

~

*T*hey were going east when Heidi spoke. "It's Tuesday."

"Uh-huh." Diego suspected what she was trying to get at.

"Aren't you supposed to be making your rounds to visit the shut-ins on Tuesdays?"

Diego nodded. She couldn't possibly come with him. He'd already decided that after much prayer. Well, he didn't exactly hear God tell him not to bring Heidi on his ministry to the elderly, but that was the point. Until he heard something, he'd better stay away from Heidi.

His plan hadn't taken off. Ming had called at noon saying he'd be running late. Could Diego pick up Heidi and take her home? Until she sold her halfway-working car, she would always need rides. She usually used Ming's car when he wasn't working, but lately, Ming had been working day and night.

When Ming called for help, Diego always responded, especially when it involved Heidi.

"I'll drop you off, and then I'll go," Diego said.

"Diego."

"What?"

"Didn't we agree to go together?"

"Not today."

"Why? You said you needed more volunteers last night. I volunteered."

"Maybe next time. Today I've got it." Diego wasn't sure what Heidi thought about his about-turn, but there they were.

"You always say that."

"Say what?"

"That you *got it*." Heidi lifted her fingers to draw quotation marks in the air. "If you don't delegate some of the ministry work, you're going to burn out sooner or later."

Diego didn't respond.

He pressed the brakes to let pedestrians cross. Downtown Savannah never slowed down. The squares were the main tourist attractions. He should have gone south toward US 80 going west, but he decided to cut through town, and here they were. Stuck in human traffic around Chippewa Square.

Stuck in the car with Heidi.

"How many seniors are you visiting this afternoon?" Heidi asked.

"Don't worry about it."

"How many?"

"Five or six."

"Should we bring them some cookies?"

Diego burst out laughing.

"What?" Heidi looked miffed.

"You remember the cookies you burned?"

"Five years ago, Diego. Of all people, you should have forgiven me."

"I have. It's just funny to think of it."

"Whatever happened to forgive and forget?"

"How can I forget your sweet gesture, although you did forget the sugar?"

Heidi lightly punched him on his arm.

"You were trying to make me feel better when Amanda walked out on me."

Silence. Then: "She didn't deserve you."

"Deserve? And who does? I'm just a plain pastor planting a church. When this church is established, it might be time for me to move on." That had been true once, but Diego didn't want it to be true anymore.

"How can you live like that?" Heidi asked.

"Live like what?"

"Moving from place to place."

"Evangelists do that all the time. They bring their families with them wherever they go."

"I can't imagine raising kids on the road, can you?"

Diego shrugged. "If God calls..."

"How do you know for sure what God has

called you to do?"

"You'll know."

"Like you know for sure that God has called you to start Riverside Chapel?"

Diego nodded. "Without a doubt, I'm supposed to be here."

Then again, if he were supposed to be here, why did Heidi feel like an obstacle to him?

Traffic cleared some, and Diego stepped on the gas pedal. The sooner he dropped off Heidi, the better.

"Without a doubt, right now I'm supposed to help you visit our elderly friends."

She is so persistent! "You're just saying that because you pity me."

"I don't pity you, Diego. I—uh—hmm... Why am I helping you?"

"I told you. It's pity."

"No. I'll find a reason soon. But now, you need to turn around. You're heading the wrong way."

Diego had to put an end to it. He pulled into a store parking lot.

"I'm glad we're turning around," Heidi said.

Diego parked the car. "We're not turning around. I can't drive and talk at the same time."

"You can't?"

"Not with you around."

Heidi's eyes widened. "I'm sorry."

"For what?"

"You said no, and I insisted. Please forgive me and take me home."

"Nothing to forgive, Heidi. I parked because I have to explain something."

"Okay."

There, in the car, with just the two of them, Diego began to speak, realizing that Heidi was in his space, his prayer closet on wheels. Here, he battled with God's will for his life. Here, he sought to do what was right for his church. Their church. Here, now, he must speak his heart so he could move on toward the upward calling of Christ.

"Heidi, you and Ming are some of my best friends in the world. You're very valuable to the growth and maturity of Riverside Chapel. I don't want to do anything to jeopardize either one of those."

"Going with you to visit some of our senior shut-ins could mess that up? I could be your *valuable* assistant."

"I don't want you to be my assistant."

"Riverside Chapel is a small church, as you said. You need all the help you can get."

Not from you, I don't.

"Am I incompetent?" Heidi asked.

"No. You're the most competent woman I know. I mean, you're accomplished—"

"Accomplished? What era are you in, Diego? Who says such things anymore?"

"I—uh…I—I mean, you…uh…"

Heidi shook her head. "I'm very surprised, Diego."

"Why?"

"You're so eloquent at the pulpit, but you can't string two words together."

"Only when I'm with you."

"Excuse me?"

"Nothing. I didn't say anything."

"You can't lie, Pastor Flores. I heard you loud and clear. Is it because I'm a woman?"

"No, no. Not that. I respect you." *Too much.* "I can never hate you, Heidi."

"Okay, then. We've known each other since college. We're buddies, right?"

"Yeah."

"Talk to me like you talk to my brother. Treat me like one of the guys. Then you won't be nervous around me."

"I don't want you to be one of the guys."

"Oh." Heidi clammed up.

"Heidi?"

No reply.

"You misunderstood me." Diego wondered what was in Heidi's mind, but she clearly looked hurt when he had said he didn't want her to be his buddy.

No.

He wanted her to be more than just one of the guys. "I want to—well, can we talk about this later?"

"You and I are different, Diego. When you have an issue, you put it off. As for me, I want to deal with it right away."

"That about sums it up."

"So we have a problem here. The lonely seniors are sitting in their rooms waiting for us to minister to them. And here we are arguing about who our best buddies are. Don't you see? On most days, those seniors sit alone, waiting for someone to call them, to visit them, to care. Would you deprive them of one more friend?"

Wow, Heidi.

Diego started the car. He reached into the car door pocket and produced a stapled printout. He handed it to Heidi. "Mrs. Untermeyer is the first person on today's list. We're bringing her tangerines. I told her I'd be praying for her. As soon as we get there, she's going to expect us to pray for her."

"Okay. Let's go."

Diego hadn't seen Heidi happier than when she was helping. Helpful Heidi, indeed.

He felt bad that he had tried to stop her from it. Perhaps it was her calling to be helpful, to minister, to give of her time to someone else in need. Perhaps God had made her that way, to find joy in helping others. Who was he to stifle that?

He had tried to be a pastor to every member of Riverside Chapel. But here, driving back toward Savannah, Diego realized that he had ministered to everyone else at church except Heidi. He had held back because of his own conflicting emotions toward her. He wanted to love her, but not the way he loved the rest of the congregation.

He wanted to love Heidi as Christ loved the church.

But now wasn't the time.

Not now, and probably not ever.

CHAPTER SIX

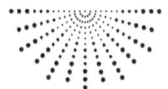

*W*hen Heidi sang "Amazing Grace" in Mandarin Chinese, it brought down the house—or the little apartment. Melvin and Marie Theroux lived here on their own without any help from anyone.

Melvin owned a poinsettia nursery, and the two of them loved Christmas. It was the reason this entire apartment was decorated with Christmas trees year round. His invalid wife, Marie, was almost eighty years old and had been bed-ridden for the better part of ten years.

Marie had grown up in Shanghai, and although Heidi had never been to Shanghai and had no relatives in China, she had taken a liking to the elderly lady who only wanted to speak to her in Mandarin

Chinese. It mattered not to her that Heidi's family was from Singapore.

Heidi wanted to give Marie a taste of home, of the East, of Asia, which Marie would probably never see again in person this side of life.

"Will you come back again?" Marie reached for Heidi.

"Yes, I will."

Marie's hand was so wrinkled and spotted that it touched Heidi's heart. She wondered whether her own mother's hand would have eventually looked like this had she been alive and grown old. As it was, Mother would never see either Heidi or Ming marry and have kids.

She wondered if Marie saw her own children and grandchildren often, but she dared not ask lest she hit an emotional nerve.

Heidi didn't have to ask Diego if he would bring her back. Now that the introductions had been made, Heidi could drive here on her own. "Tell me what songs you'd like me to sing next time."

"'Amazing Grace.' You can sing that as many times as you want, Little Peony."

Little Peony?

Nearby, Melvin covered his mouth with his hand.

"Are you all right, sir?" Diego asked.

"My wife called her Little Peony," Melvin translated. "That's the name of our little baby girl who died a few days after Marie gave birth to her during the war."

The war?

"Which war?" Heidi asked.

"Second World War."

"I'm sorry." Diego spoke to Melvin, but all the time he was looking at Heidi. He picked up his guitar again. "Let's sing one more song. How about it, Heidi?"

Heidi managed a smile. "What would you like to hear, Marie?"

"'I'm a Little Teapot,'" she said in English. "I want Little Peony and me to sing it together."

"A duet. I'll be glad to, Marie." Heidi turned to Diego. "We can do that, can't we?"

"Sure." Diego swiped his iPhone to get the guitar chords.

So began Heidi's song. She finished the nursery rhyme, standing behind Diego with her hands on his shoulders, all of them laughing and singing the refrain. Marie kept on singing, and Diego plucked his guitar again to keep up with the lady.

A prayer and a goodbye later, Heidi was still humming the nursery rhyme when Diego put his guitar in the backseat of the car. He seemed to be looking at her more in the last hour or so, but Heidi tried to brush it off.

"I can't believe we did that." Diego started the car.

"All things to all people, you mean?"

"We'll never live down the teapot song." Diego merged into traffic. "You survived all five visits this afternoon."

"I had fun."

"I did too."

"Aren't you glad I came along?" Heidi asked.

"Very glad." He glanced over at Heidi. "Are you crying?"

Heidi wiped her eyes. "I want to visit Marie again."

"You can visit her anytime. I'll give you their number. I won't be back for a couple of weeks."

"Why not sooner?"

"To be fair to everyone. At the time we're visiting Marie, someone else is sitting alone, waiting for us to stop by to talk with them, pray with them. Marie has Melvin. Some others... Their spouses have died long ago, and their children are too far away to visit."

"How many seniors are on your list?"

"About twenty shut-ins."

"We need more volunteers." Heidi tapped the armrest as Diego headed for Tybee Island to drop her off.

"What I said." Diego chuckled.

"I'll talk to my brother."

"Don't. He's busy."

"Too busy to serve God?"

"Heidi."

"What?"

"Don't be too hard on your brother. He serves God in other ways."

"Sure. Like getting shot and killed is a way to serve God?"

Diego was silent. Then: "That's so unlike you to be angry."

"I'm just upset."

"It's difficult to see people get old and wither away, but Marie has Melvin, and he's going strong even at eighty-nine years old."

"Melvin is eighty-nine?" Heidi was shocked. "No way. He looked like he's in his seventies."

"Well, it's a good thing they still have each other."

"And they have God," Heidi offered.

"Melvin, yes, but Marie, I'm not so sure."

"What do you mean? She prayed with us." Heidi swiped her iPhone to check when she could go back to see Marie. Her entire week was booked. Maybe she could rearrange some of her project meetings at CGU and docent work at the Museum of Coastal Georgia History.

She felt too tired to do it now, but she made a mental note to work that in later.

"Just because Marie prayed with us, it doesn't mean she is saved," Diego said. "You know that."

"I suppose so, but surely you have more information than that."

"Melvin said that he didn't remember if Marie ever received Jesus Christ as her personal Lord and Savior." Diego coasted down US Highway 80 by the Savannah River toward the Atlantic Ocean.

The sun was still up in the sky, but it was past Heidi's dinnertime. Her stomach rumbled. Seemed like that chicken salad she had for lunch had worn off.

"Hungry?" Diego asked.

"Just a little."

"How about dinner?"

"I'll have some when I get home."

"I mean somewhere."

Heidi raised an eyebrow. *Diego and me?*

"Just dinner."

Heidi mulled it over. She was exhausted. She wasn't dressed to go for dinner. She was in the same clothes she had on when she had left the house at seven o'clock this morning. Dinner with Diego? Not today.

"Maybe another time?" Heidi asked. "I'm tired."

"Me too. Rain check, then."

Diego turned into Ming's driveway and parked. Ming's car wasn't there. As per usual, Heidi got out of the car herself. She was surprised that Diego had stepped out of the car too.

He stood there so long that it made Heidi worried. "You okay?"

"Don't get me wrong about dinner." Diego walked toward Heidi. "I didn't...wasn't trying to..."

"We'll be two friends having dinner, right?" Heidi smiled. "It's not like we're going to suddenly hold hands and kiss, you know."

"You mean like this?" He locked his fingers into Heidi's, leaned down, and kissed her on the—

Forehead!

Heidi smiled warmly. "I think you missed."

"Huh?"

"Next time, don't miss." She tilted up her head, and kissed him on the—

Cheek.

~

*W*ow, Heidi.

Diego nearly ran over Ming's mailbox on his way out of the driveway. How embarrassing. His mind was preoccupied with Heidi. All Heidi.

She was Helping Heidi who had visited the

elderly with him all afternoon without a complaint. She had sung hymns beautifully, even doing duets with him a couple of times. He should teach her "Amazing Grace" in Spanish and Italian. He wasn't very good in Italian himself, as Mom had spoken more Spanish to him and his brothers when they were growing up. Someday he'd go to Italy and attend church with his cousins.

Meanwhile, he had Riverside Chapel to worry about.

Not worry, Lord. Sorry.

The church had grown steadily. God had always provided them with a place to meet and people to minister. Today was another example of God's provision.

Five hours, five shut-ins served.

"Lord, I pray You will redeem the time that Heidi spent ministering to our dear friends." Diego drove off Tybee Island. He knew she had a dissertation to complete. And yet she had chosen to spend the time doing the Lord's work. Surely God would see that and reward her for it.

And then she was Happy Heidi claiming he had missed a kiss. She had proven it with her own missed kiss.

How did he feel about that?

Miserable.

Really, he hadn't missed. He had deliberately

not kissed her on the lips to prove he wasn't trying to take advantage of her. Yet she had shown, with her correction of him, that she had feelings for him.

Five years.

It had taken five years to come to this point.

And now Diego didn't know what to do.

Should I tell her how I feel?

He enjoyed Heidi's company and would like to know her more. However, he had a church to pastor and wouldn't have time to give to Heidi. His mind felt divided.

"I don't want my relationship with Heidi to only be platonic," Diego said aloud. "Lord, what to do? What to do?"

CHAPTER SEVEN

"*I*'ll be back in a couple of hours." Heidi stuffed her stash of printouts and a sweater into her backpack. The campus library was always cold, regardless of time of day. Truly, Heidi would prefer solo independent studies, but this group research project would benefit the Coastal Georgia Historical Society, and she was willing to do her bit for history's sake.

After all, what are historians for?

Ming put away his iPhone in his back jeans pocket, looked up at his sister, and tried to appear nonchalant.

Heidi knew that look. "Uh-oh."

"Uh-oh what?"

"Don't do this to me."

"Do what? It's just a job. I'll be home before you get up."

"Five o'clock?"

"If you get up before I get home, say a prayer for me, and cook me some pancakes, will you?" Ming pulled out his car keys. "Lock the doors and set the alarm."

"If I do that, it'll go off when you try to get in." Heidi watched the old clock on the wall. Any minute now her ride would be honking outside.

"I'll call you first." For some reason, Ming hugged her.

When Heidi put her arms around her brother, she felt the metal bulge tucked into his jeans at his spine. She hated it. Hated it with all her heart. Hated all the Glocks and Sig Sauers that Ming kept in the house. But this was his house. She was his tenant.

"I don't like your job," Heidi said. "If Mom were alive, she'd have a heart attack."

Ming laughed. "I'm working with Cam. You trust Cam."

Heidi nodded.

"So trust me. Trust God to protect me. We're never alone, sis. God is always with us. No worries."

"Why do you have to work at night?" Heidi's voice broke. "Following people around and all. Let someone else do it. Oh, listen to me. That sounds selfish."

"You don't want me to get hurt." Ming hugged her again. "I don't blame you. You can pray for me. God hears our prayers."

Heidi nodded. Outside the house, a car honked.

"It's a job. When my company grows, I'll hire people and I'll stop doing night shifts."

"Promise?" Heidi grabbed her backpack and headed for the front door. "I have to go. Promise?"

"Promise. Don't forget my pancakes!" Ming stood there in the middle of the small living room.

Heidi tried to save that scene in her memory. Her only brother, who meant everything to her in all the world, standing there looking at her with compassion, with their mother's eyes and their father's face.

~

*H*eidi slept fitfully all night. What if something happened to Ming? What was she going to do?

She woke up several times. She tried to pray, but she had no words. She ended up reading the Bible. Psalms. Lots and lots of Psalms. She fell back asleep on the bed with the open Bible on her stomach.

A distant barking dog awakened Heidi. The

sounds of the surf in their backyard and a few squawks of seabirds told her it was morning. She opened her eyes, groggy from the interrupted sleep pattern all night.

Her Bible had slid down her tummy to the mattress. She picked it up and read a few verses. She closed her eyes and prayed for Ming as he had asked.

Then she remembered he also wanted pancakes.

She glanced at her iPhone.

Six o'clock!

She had overslept by an hour.

Heidi jumped out of bed, brushed her teeth quickly, and hopped into the shower. She wrapped her wavy chest-length hair in a dry beach towel and padded down the hallway to the small galley kitchen.

"Ming!" She opened her arms wide, ran toward Ming at the kitchen sink, and hugged him from behind.

"Ouch!" Ming turned around.

Heidi shrieked. "What happened to your face?"

It was red and raw in spots on his cheeks and forehead. There was a bandage over his ears.

"No worries, sis."

"That's when I get really worried."

Ming limped toward the stove. "I made you pancakes."

"I'm supposed to do that for you."

"You didn't wake up at five o'clock."

"I hardly slept all night from worries. You have no idea how many times I prayed for you." Heidi tried not to cry, but the tears just flowed, bursting forth from a whole night of bottling them up.

Ming gathered her in his arms. Gently.

Too gently, Heidi thought. She wondered how extensive his injuries were.

"Promise me there'll be no more such late nights," Heidi said.

"I told you, Heidi. It's part of the job. Look, I'm still alive."

"By God's mercy."

"Sure. He's taking care of me."

"But you're tempting death, Ming. What do you think our parents would say?"

"They're dead."

"God then? What do you think God would say about your reckless lifestyle?"

Ming looked angry. "Reckless? I paid for these pancakes, and you call me reckless? I paid for this house you slept in last night. I paid for—hey, where are you going?"

"To pack and move out." Heidi ran out of the kitchen.

CHAPTER EIGHT

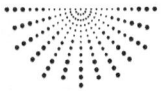

"Y ou can stay here as long as you want."
Abilene Dupree handed Heidi a
blanket and a pillow.

Heidi hated having to ask her friend from
church for help, but hotels were expensive in the
Savannah area. She needed a place to stay for a
couple of days to think about what to do next. Her
brother's insults, warranted or otherwise, were
wearing her down.

She had to graduate and get out of his hair, but it
was only September, and graduation wasn't until
December.

"I'm sorry that all I have are my couches, but I
can assure you they're very comfortable, and you'll
probably fall asleep on them right away."

Heidi nodded. "Thank you, Abilene."

After all these years, she had finally left her brother's house. It felt like it was past time. She had hung around him after their parents passed away, and the months had turned into years. Whether she and Ming had needed each other equally or whether she needed Ming more, she couldn't tell.

All she knew was that she finally left. She wished it hadn't been on such poor terms with Ming, not when she had waited all night for him to come home.

God had answered her prayer; Ming was alive, albeit beaten up a bit. Why wasn't she grateful?

Why wasn't Ming grateful?

The doorbell rang. It was Nadine, back from her two-week vacation on the West Coast. The three friends hugged.

"What's wrong, Heidi?" Nadine asked. She was wearing a tank top that showed off the tan on her shoulders and arms.

"Her brother," Abilene answered for Heidi.

"Oh. Want me to talk to him? I'll slap some sense into him. Whatever he needs."

Heidi chuckled at Nadine's brazenness. "No need, sweet friend. I'll handle it."

"He's too cute for his own good."

"Nadine!" Heidi and Abilene said together.

"I'm serious. Is he still single?"

"You've only been gone two weeks, Nadine.

Nothing much has changed." In fact, nothing much had changed in years. Ming was still the bossy big brother, and if anyone asked Ming, he'd say she was the bossy little sister. Like they said, it took one to know one.

"Are we just going to stand here and mope, or are we going to lunch?" Nadine waved her iPhone around. It said 11:30 a.m. "We'll barely beat the lunch crowd. Piper's Place is usually packed on Fridays."

"Did you say mope? Who's moping?" Abilene ushered everyone out.

"I think she meant me," Heidi said.

"Yes, I did." Nadine gave her a hug and a squeeze. "Your lunch is on me, okay?"

"There's no need."

"I insist." Nadine clicked on her keychain remote. The car doors unlocked. "Ming gets on my nerves sometimes, but I don't have to live with him. You do."

"Well, I'm bunking with Abilene here for a few days."

Nadine scrunched up her nose. "You asked Abilene for a place to stay, but you didn't ask me."

"You just got home."

"I'm your friend too. Tell you what. Why don't you stay with both of us? When Abilene's tired of you, move in with me."

"I'll never be tired of Heidi," Abilene said.

"Neither will I."

Heidi was moved. "Such nice friends you are. Let me think about it. Either way I graduate in December."

"How does it feel to finally move out of your brother's shadow?" Nadine asked. "Emaciated?"

Heidi laughed so hard she almost bashed her head against Nadine's car door as she climbed in. "You mean *emancipated.*"

"Gotcha. Feel better?" Nadine raised her eyebrows.

Heidi wiped tears from her eyes. "I love y'all."

CHAPTER NINE

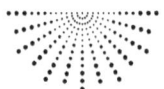

*S*aturday was the day Diego slept in, but not today. Events had moved quickly, and divine doors of opportunity had opened and shut outside his control. If he missed this one, he missed it altogether. He doubted it'd come around again.

God had given Riverside Chapel a new church venue, complete with small dining and meeting rooms that could be used for Sunday school classes and a nursery for the children. They were all there for his taking.

Free of charge.

He couldn't ask for anything more.

God had opened this door for him, for his congregation.

So here he was. Eyes closed, body flat on his

bed, unable to even reach for the blasting alarm clock on the dresser. Yes, dresser. It was at least ten feet away from his bed for a reason.

He fell asleep thinking about getting up.

Five minutes later, he rolled out of bed and headed for the dresser to turn off the alarm clock.

On the way, he passed by his guitar case and remembered Heidi and their Tuesday afternoon together. It had been more than three days since then, but it was still fresh in his mind. The way she had sung with him made his day. The way she had asked to return to visit the Therouxes touched his heart.

All that had happened because he had been flexible with God's plans. At least he thought that had been God's plan. As for his own plan, Diego had been determined to avoid Heidi.

Just in case something happened between them.

Sure enough, it had happened.

Diego couldn't remember when he had started to notice Heidi back at the University of Georgia. She had hung out with Ming and the guys, and to Diego she had always been there, more so after her parents suddenly passed away.

Back then, Diego had majored in accounting. He had started on his MBA program, also at UGA. It had been on numerous mission trips all over the world that he felt the calling to leave UGA and go to seminary instead.

Does my being a pastor hinder Heidi from—

What am I talking about?

We're just friends!

Diego dragged himself into his small bathroom and squeezed a blob of toothpaste onto his toothbrush. He wondered whether Heidi rolled up the toothpaste from the bottom of the tube like he did. Or did she make a mess of it?

Half an hour later, he made himself a plate of eggs and hash browns with shredded cheddar on top. The coffee was hot, the breakfast was delicious, but he ate alone.

Alone.

Always alone.

Does Heidi feel alone too?

It was then that Diego remembered he had forgotten to read the Bible.

Wow, Heidi.

This could be bad if his thoughts of Heidi had prevented him from spending time in God's word. Still, he hadn't forgotten it entirely, so it was a good thing.

Fifty minutes late wasn't too bad.

He swiped his iPad and went on to the next Psalm on his reading list. He read Psalm 86 aloud, his eyes revisiting some verses afterward.

Psalm 86:10–13 rose from the screen.

For You are great, and do wondrous things;
   You alone are God.
   Teach me Your way, O Lord;
   I will walk in Your truth;
   Unite my heart to fear Your name.
   I will praise You, O Lord my God, with all my
heart,
   And I will glorify Your name forevermore.
   For great is Your mercy toward me,
   And You have delivered my soul from the
depths of Sheol.*

Yes, indeed. God has saved my soul forevermore.

Diego began praying for his small congregation, from the littlest baby to the oldest adult member of Riverside Chapel. Then he prayed for all the people outside the church whom he visited. He remembered Marie Theroux, whose salvation was questionable.

And Marie reminded him of Heidi.

Again.

"O Lord, help me. I know You have called me to pastor Riverside Chapel for such a time as this. When this church is thriving, then it's time for me to move on to plant another church somewhere else. Such is my calling. Help me not to be distracted from that which You have called me to do. It might be that I have to be single the rest of my life to accomplish the task of starting and establishing new churches across North America. Help me not to deviate from Your plan for my life."

What did I just pray?

Oh well. What was said was said.

"In Jesus' Name I pray. Amen." Diego finished his breakfast, rinsed off the plate, and put it in the dishwasher.

He locked the door and left the house. The riverboat was twenty minutes away from his apartment. Several of his church members had agreed to meet at the riverboat with buckets, mops, and rags.

Yes, Heidi would be there. And if she was Helpful Heidi as she had been, then Diego knew she'd be doing an immense amount of work, probably more than anyone else. He'd have to step in to stop her from overexerting herself and doing everyone else's job.

He let out a laugh. "Who am I to talk? I'm the one who doesn't know how to delegate."

CHAPTER TEN

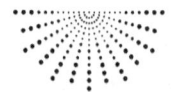

*R*iver Street was not crowded when he coasted down the cobblestone road. The city of Savannah was still sleeping from Friday night's partying, the sun was rising and doing its usual thing, and the river was still flowing brown from all the river traffic.

I love this place!

Diego parked at his usual spot in a public parking lot some two blocks away from the storefront where Riverside Chapel had met for Sunday services. The landlord had raised the rates again, and when the rental came up for renewal, it would be difficult to afford that location anymore. That had been one of the biggest reasons Diego was confident the free riverboat was a gift from God.

For however long it lasted, free was free.

There was no shame for a church to accept charitable gifts.

Diego walked eight blocks past a row of hotels and shops, past the visitors' center and more shops. He crossed the road and took a picture of the riverboat on his iPhone. He sent it to Dad with a note on iMessage.

Bet you didn't get such an opportunity back when you pastored churches.

A few minutes later, his iPhone pinged.

"Son, I don't bet." Diego laughed as he read it aloud. He texted back.

Figure of speech, Dad.

Diego trekked up the ramp to the door of the riverboat. Jerome had given him the keys to the entire place. He put down his cleaning supplies on the wooden floor, and found the keys in his pocket. He unlocked the door.

It smelled musty in the retro-style dining room. Echoing the 1920s, he thought.

Diego was opening windows, when his phone rang.

"Hey, Dad." Diego was always happy to talk with his parents. They were on an extended vacation visiting Mom's relatives in Sorrento, Italy. The vacation had begun with a monthlong visit right after Christmas. They'd stayed through the summer. Now it was September, and there was no sign that the Reverend and Mrs. Samuel Flores would ever come home, especially since they had taken their pug with them.

"Mom wants to know if you ate breakfast."

Are you kidding me?

Diego shook his head. Here he was, an ordained pastor of a church, and Mom wanted to know if he had eaten breakfast. Still, Mom was Mom. He listed all the things he had eaten that morning for breakfast.

He almost added that at twenty-nine years old, he knew not to starve, but he decided not to make those snide remarks that had come easily to him back when he was in high school. He had been quite rebellious, hurting and cutting Mom with his words.

Funny how it had taken him more than ten years to bridle his tongue.

Mom had meant well.

She had always meant well.

Diego hadn't seen it when he was young and immature. He'd grown up in college and at seminary.

"Mom wants to talk with you," Dad said.

"Sure. Always glad to hear her voice."

"I'm glad you do, Son. Good to hear that. She's not feeling too well today, so be nice, okay?"

It hurt to hear Dad remind him of days gone by, days Diego could never retrieve or redeem. The grace of God was deeper than his own sins, but oh, how it hurt to remember those times when he had been unkind to Mom when she needed his support. The times when Dad had been busy preaching three Sunday morning and one Sunday evening services, and another Wednesday night service, it was up to Diego and his brothers to provide the encouragement that Mom needed through her times alone.

But Diego hadn't been there.

He had failed to minister to the one woman in the world who needed him most at that time.

He could say that Dad's shoes were too big for him to fill.

He could say that he had older brothers and it had been more their jobs than his.

He could say countless things.

However, he could not rewind time and roll back all those spiteful words that had spewed out of his sassy mouth. James 3:8–10 came to his mind. He had preached that a few times in the year.

> But no man can tame the tongue. It is an unruly evil, full of deadly poison. With it we bless our God and Father, and with it we curse men, who have been made in the similitude of God. Out of the same mouth proceed blessing and cursing. My brethren, these things ought not to be so.

How ironic it was that God had called him into ministry. It had taken four years for God to clean out his mouth and infuse him with words of blessing and not cursing, words of life and not death, words of peace and not war.

"Don't listen to your dad." Mom's sweet voice reached Diego's ear. "I'm not sick. I have a bit of a cold. That's all."

"Did you see the doctor?"

"This morning."

"And?"

"He said I have a cold."

"Just want to be sure it's only a cold."

Mom laughed, and then coughed something fierce. "You worry too much, Diego."

"I love you, Mom."

"I know. I love you too."

"Go to bed early. Get a lot of rest." Diego realized he was worried.

"And call you in the morning?"

"I'll be praying for you, Mom."

"Thank you. We need all the prayer we can get. I don't think your dad is ever going to leave this place. As much as I love seeing my cousins and people I didn't even know are related to me, I want to go home. I don't know how long my neighbor wants to keep watering my plants for me in Irvine."

Home.

Mom had been born in a small town outside Sorrento, but grew up in Canada, and met and married Dad when they were both still in college. A passel of kids later, they had continued to live in Irvine even after all their children had left town.

"Do you have a girlfriend yet?" Mom asked.

Her question took him by surprise.

He heard noises and laughter. He turned to look. Heidi was coming his way with Nadine and Abilene. Heidi looked pretty with her hair tied up in a chignon on the top of her head.

Did I say pretty?

They waved to him.

Over the phone, Mom repeated her question.

"Uh, no. Not right now."

Mom sighed so loudly that Diego could hear her all the way across the Tyrrhenian Sea and the North Atlantic Ocean.

"I want at least two grandkids. Remember that, Diego."

"You already have fourteen."

"Two more, dear. A boy and a girl, preferably."

"I'll pray about it." Diego knew his response was a cop-out.

Lord, forgive me.

He was still on the phone when the three ladies went to work. They had rags in their hands, wiping down tables, chattering as they went. Heidi was coming out of the broom closet, pushing a vacuum cleaner.

"Mom, I'm at the riverboat, doing some cleaning. I'll call you another time?"

"All right. When do you start services there?"

"By the first week of October, I hope."

"Yes, I heard about the new rent at the storefront. That's crazy. Anything we can do to help?"

"Thanks for the offer, Mom, but the riverboat rent is free."

"All the more reason to thank God for your new church location."

"Yes. As soon as we get this place cleaned up and all the paperwork done, I'll let you know. You and Dad can make plans to attend a service here."

"Good!" She sounded excited. "I can't wait. Go clean up the place."

"We're doing it now."

"I'll let you go. And, Diego?"

"What, Mom?"

"Two kids. Don't forget."

Diego chuckled. "Talk with you later, Mom. You have a good afternoon over there, okay?"

Six hours of time difference.

Diego chided himself for not calling his parents more often. He had been preoccupied with church. And when he wasn't thinking of church and sermons and ministry, he was thinking of—

"Good morning, Diego," Heidi said.

"Morning." He suddenly recalled that Tuesday afternoon when he had dropped her off at her house. He couldn't remember what had overcome him to cause him to hold her hands. He liked the way her hands fitted into his.

More than I should.

CHAPTER ELEVEN

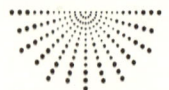

hy did Diego look at me like that?

Heidi thought that he seemed half-glad to see her this morning, but the rest of him seemed unhappy that they were in the same room. Why? Was it because of what had happened on Tuesday?

She regretted how that day had ended. She had been forward with him outside her brother's house, and tried to teach him a lesson.

It wasn't her place. She realized it now, four days too late.

Heidi dragged the vacuum cleaner toward the carpet, passing by Diego and Nadine talking.

Did Diego know about her tiff with Ming? Surely Ming had spoken to him about it. Ming always aired their family problems in front of Diego.

Heidi suspected Diego knew everything about the Wei family—all two members of it—and its broken pieces.

Heidi didn't think that her relationship with Ming was fractured.

No. Only tense.

Maybe it was because they were stubborn.

Maybe even bossy.

Bossy.

Wasn't that what Diego had called her and Ming?

She saw Diego walk out the door with his bucket. He started mopping outside where the deck was overlooking the Savannah River and the waterfront. She turned off her vacuum cleaner and walked toward him.

He saw her coming. "Watch out. Wet floor."

Heidi kept walking. "Is everything okay?"

"What do you mean?"

"Between us?"

"More than okay—I mean, yes." His face straightened. "We're fine."

"Then why are you frowning? Have you spoken with my brother?"

"About what?" The loud voice was Ming's coming from behind them.

Heidi turned to find her brother striding up the ramp.

His right elbow was bandaged. Dried blood was on his arm.

Uh-oh.

Heidi's jaw dropped.

"Ming! What happened?" She cupped Ming's elbow in her hands. "Unbelievable! What have you done now, Ming?"

"Careful there. It hurts."

Heidi began to cry softly.

"No worries, sis." Ming pushed away a loose strand of hair from Heidi's forehead.

Diego was in front of them now. "What do you mean no worries, Ming? Look at you. This has got to stop."

"This what?" Ming asked, obviously amused.

"This fight club thing or whatever."

"Fight club?" Heidi's eyes grew large.

"Don't listen to him," Ming said. "He's just kidding. There's no fight club. I was working with Cam, and things got a bit rough at the job site. If you think this is bad, you should see Cam. He's black and blue all over. He threw himself in front of me."

"Brave Cam. Is he all right?" Heidi asked.

Diego scowled.

Heidi had never seen him scowl like that before.

"He's fine," Ming said. "He's sitting in the car waiting, so I have to go. I came to tell you I can't help clean the church today."

"That's all right," Diego said.

"I came to see you, sis." Ming wrapped his good arm around Heidi.

"Tell you what, Ming," Diego said. "Let me pray for you and Cam right now. For safety."

Ming nodded. The trio held hands.

Diego's hand felt warm in Heidi's. She couldn't stop the tears. Pretty soon Diego's arm was around her. She felt his care, but more than that, she felt his prayers.

He was all pastor now.

His prayer was strong and sure and full of faith.

Heidi realized then that she could not possibly carry on anything with this man of God. He was above her. So much above her. Sure, she had been saved since high school, but it seemed that she had a long way to go in terms of spiritual maturity.

Oh, to be able to pray like that. To pray with certainty that God heard her prayers.

"Amen," Diego finished.

Heidi slid out from under Diego's arm, telling herself that he had put his arm on her during the prayer time because he felt sorry for her weak faith. It wasn't weak to cry, but when it came to Ming, Heidi felt helpless to stop her brother from taking unnecessary risks and hurting himself in the process.

What was she going to do if something

happened to Ming? If he died? Or if he was so badly injured that he became paralyzed?

"Ming, please." Heidi tugged at Ming's short sleeve.

"No worries, Sis. I told you." He hugged her. "Listen, I have to run. Cam's going to get a ticket. I left my car key on the kitchen table in case you need a car. I'll be home by midnight."

"Promise?"

"I'm going to try."

"Is there a way to contact you in case of an emergency?" Heidi knew what the answer was, but she had to ask anyway.

"No. We go dark, and no one can know our whereabouts. Have to keep the witness in—I can't say more. You want us to be safe, don't you?"

Heidi nodded. "If anything happens..."

Ming slapped Diego's shoulder. "This is the guy to call. He's also the executor of my will."

Heidi gasped.

"No worries, Sis. It's just a precaution. You should update your will too, you know. Leave me everything."

"Don't talk like that. Come back, Ming."

"Of course. Who's going to grill your favorite salmon burger if I don't come back to do it?" Ming laughed. "Diego here is useless at the grill."

"Hey!" Diego frowned.

"I'm telling the truth. You can't even start the grill."

"It's charcoal, man. I can handle a gas grill just fine."

"Anyone can handle a gas grill. See? I rest my case."

"Send someone else," Heidi said to Ming.

"I will next time. This is my last job with Cam. He might get promoted on this."

"Or you might both be killed."

Everyone was quiet.

Ming spoke first after the moment of silence.

"Listen, Sis. Will you come back to the house? I'm sorry about all the garbage I said yesterday."

To Diego, Ming said, "You keep an eye on her, will you? I don't want her coming after me or anything of that sort."

"Will do," Diego said. "You take care. Don't forget the verse I gave you the other day."

"Deuteronomy 31:8. Got it." Ming walked away from Heidi and Diego.

And the Lord, He is the One who goes before you.
He will be with you, He will not leave you nor
forsake you; do not fear nor be dismayed.

Heidi went to the edge of the balcony to see

Ming go. As he walked across the esplanade and to the sidewalk, he didn't look back.

Up on River Street, a police officer on a bicycle was talking to Camden La Salle at his car. Ming ran toward his friend as the officer pedaled away.

And then the two men were off.

Gone down the street with a chunk of Heidi's heart.

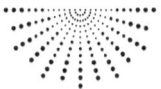

hat in the world is Ming doing that he can't even tell his sister?

Diego wondered how to handle the Wei family situation as he stood next to Heidi on the deck. They stared across the waterfront to the empty spot on the street where Camden's car had been parked a minute ago. River Street carried on, with pedestrians and vehicles going this way and that.

"The next time I see Cam, I'm going to have a good talk with him," Heidi said. "I don't care how much the Feds are paying my brother. It can't be worth all that trouble."

"Why don't you let me talk to Cam?" Diego said. He had a bit more information than he could tell Heidi. The night before, Ming had emailed him some emergency numbers. Diego prayed he never had to reread the email. He wanted Ming back home safely as much as Heidi did. Perhaps more than she did. He couldn't bear to see her looking sad.

"I can handle it. Cam and I dated once, remember?"

"I do remember." Diego didn't want to drag out the memories, but Camden and Heidi had met at Riverside Chapel, in that dinky storefront he had rented for Sunday morning services. With no more than three dozen members back then, it wasn't hard to know all that was going on among the congregation.

"I suppose you do since you're our pastor."

I want to be more than your pastor, Heidi.

But I can't.

"We prayed, right?" Diego said. "We asked God to protect Ming and Cam. Let's put our faith in God, not in people."

Heidi nodded.

Diego used the pad of his thumb to wipe a trickle of tear on Heidi's cheek.

"Sorry." He quickly stuffed his hands into his pockets.

"I'm the one who should be sorry." Heidi's dark-brown eyes were intent on his.

"For what?"

"For Tuesday."

"Tuesday?" So many things happened on Tuesday.

"I didn't mean to, uh"—Heidi glanced around—"to, you know, respond like that."

"I've wanted to do that for a very long time."

"Seriously?"

"Five years, Heidi."

"No way. You never said a word."

"I had no word to say to you. Besides, you were always with someone. Cam, for instance."

"Cam? That was over a long time ago. It was a whirlwind relationship."

"Sixteen to seventeen months ago."

"Has it been that long?"

"Then there were all those guys you brought to our church."

"You noticed."

Diego nodded slightly. He was embarrassed now that he had been a fly on the wall, watching Heidi come and go with her ex-boyfriends, never getting a chance to tell her how much he—

What?

How much I what?

I can't.

"We'd better get back to cleaning." Heidi put her hand on his arm.

She did that a lot, and Diego liked the way their skin touched.

I shouldn't.

At all.

"I'm sorry, Diego—Pastor Flores."

"Diego. I will always be Diego to you. We knew each other long before I was called into ministry."

"I—we can't."

"Can't what?"

"Just can't. I don't want to get in the way of God's calling for your life."

"Neither do I."

"Glad we agree."

It hurts. But we both know we can't mess this up.

"Riverside Chapel has to thrive," Diego said. "We can't let anything personal get in the way of corporate worship."

"You know, I've often wondered about that word."

"What word?"

"Corporate." Heidi tipped her head. "Don't you think it makes more sense to call it *congregational* rather than *corporate* worship? The church is not a company."

"You know, you're right, Heidi. I won't use that phrase again. Thank you." Diego had nothing but admiration for her.

Stop staring!

Heidi looked uncomfortable now.

Diego started backing away. "I'd better get back

to mopping, and you to vacuuming. The church isn't going to clean itself."

"Right. Only God can cleanse His church."

Diego was startled.

Only God can cleanse His church.

Heidi had said it nonchalantly, but there was so much truth in her statement that he could make a whole sermon series out of it. "Sometimes you say the most profound things."

"I say what I see. And right now I don't see anything good coming out of Ming's friendship with Cam. I think it's going to end badly."

Oh. Her mind is still on Ming and Cam.

"God will keep them safe," Diego said.

"What was that verse you gave my brother?"

"Deuteronomy 31:8."

"Okay. I can look it up."

"Do that later, but I can tell you what it is. 'And the Lord, He is the One who goes before you. He will be with you, He will not leave you nor forsake you; do not fear nor be dismayed.' I've got this verse memorized because I needed it myself."

"I should memorize it too. I fear—I try not to, but yes, I do fear."

"No need to fear, Heidi. God is already there. Ahead of you, with you, in you. And He's your rear guard as well."

"Thank you, Diego."

"I'll email you some more verses, if you like."

"Please do," Heidi said. "I really need to memorize more verses. I do underline them as I read my Bible, but I don't always memorize them."

"That's a good start. When we need God's Word, the Holy Spirit brings the passages of Scripture to our minds to comfort us and carry us forward. But if we don't know the verses, how can He help us recall that which we haven't remembered in our hearts?"

Heidi smiled. "Diego."

"What?"

"You'll never cease to be a teaching pastor, will you?"

"I'm not going to apologize. It's not only my job. It's who I am."

"Never apologize." Heidi seemed to calm down now. Her tears were gone. The brightness in her eyes was returning.

Diego liked what he saw. "Do you want another verse?"

"Sure."

"Psalm 56:3 says, 'Whenever I am afraid, I will trust in You.' Before you even fear, trust God."

"Pre-trust?"

"You can say that if it helps you remember the verse," Diego replied. "God is all you need, Heidi."

And God is all I need too.

CHAPTER THIRTEEN

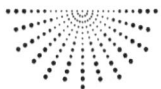

*S*hortly after two o'clock in the morning, Heidi and a groggy Abilene drove to Ming's house. It was dark all around the porch. All Heidi heard were the noise of the Atlantic waves crashing against the beach behind the house, and some insects in the bushes. There were no other sounds. No street noise, no cars, no owls.

Heidi unlocked the front door. A slice of silver moonlight shone in through the back windows and lit part of the kitchen and living room, but it was gone quickly, probably blocked by clouds in the sky. Heidi's hand groped the wall and found the switch. She flicked on the living room light.

After Abilene stepped inside the house, Heidi locked and bolted the door behind her. She went to the kitchen. There it was, a single key on the counter. Below the car key was a note. A scrawl, really, as Ming didn't have the best penmanship in the Wei family. The handwriting accolades had almost always gone to Heidi, though these days she preferred to type.

The note was brief. Ming had never been one to speak much. Heidi sniffled.

"What is it?" Abilene yawned. Her hair was all askew. She tried to hold it down, but her curls sprang straight up into the air.

Heidi was sorry she had woken up her friend to drive her to Tybee Island to check on her brother. Well, her suspicions were correct. Ming wasn't home. Heidi had persistently called since midnight, when he had said he'd be home. After texting, messaging, and leaving him voice mail, she had felt an urgent need to come out here.

Heidi pushed the note toward Abilene. There was nothing on there but something Ming said to her all the time.

"No worries, sis," Abilene read aloud.

"I'm going to stay here tonight." Heidi was sure she wasn't going to get any sleep at all. "Thank you for driving me. If you go home now, you'll be there in twenty minutes and you can sleep in your own bed."

"I'm not leaving you here by yourself."

"Thanks, but I'll be okay. Ming has left me his

car key, so if I need to leave in a hurry, I can do that."

"You mean if someone calls you and says he's in the hospital?" Abilene asked.

Heidi nodded. "I hope it won't get to that."

"Usually we think of that as the worst-case scenario."

"The morgue would be the worst-case scenario," Heidi said. "Reminds me of the kinds of call we got when our parents died."

Abilene went around the table and hugged Heidi. "I'm so sorry."

"Ming is all I have."

"You have me, and Nadine, God, of course, and —I guess you also have Pastor Flores." Abilene made a face. "You guys were chatting while we did all the menial labor this morning on the riverboat."

"No, we didn't! Ming came, and we had to deal with him, but after that Diego mopped and I vacuumed. We worked."

"What's with you two?"

"Nothing's going on."

"Uh-huh." Abilene went to the refrigerator. "Do you have any mineral water?"

"Bottom shelf."

"I see. Want some?"

"No, thanks. I'll make some coffee."

Ten minutes later they were sitting down in the

living room. Neither one could sleep. Heidi reached for the Bible on the side table. She had bought it for the living room to remind herself to read the Bible. There were several bookmarks sticking out of the pages, but she went for the verses that Diego had shared with her on Saturday morning.

"Ming knows this verse. Shall I read it to us?" Heidi asked.

"What is it?" Abilene was sprawled out on the other couch. It was then that Heidi realized her friend was wearing pajamas. There had been no time to change and pretty up when they had been in such a hurry to get over here to wait.

"Deuteronomy 31:8."

"Okay. Go."

And the Lord, He is the One who goes before you. He will be with you, He will not leave you nor forsake you; do not fear nor be dismayed.

Abilene seemed to approve. "Sounds like something we all can use."

"Sure thing. I'm assuming this verse implies that we're going in the right direction. God wouldn't lead us into a path of destruction. In fact, He tries to protect us from destruction."

"Yep."

"The proof of that is the rest of the verse. God

will be with us. He will not fail us. He will not forsake us."

"Right."

"Our point of failure is when we pivot in the wrong direction and go off sinning. God goes one way, and we go another."

"Sometimes even in the opposite route."

Heidi nodded. "Did we just learn something new?"

"The Holy Spirit teaches Christians the Word of God."

"So we have here a statement of who God is and what He will do." Heidi relaxed. "And the last part of the verse tells us what we need to do. Do not fear. Do not be dismayed."

"Or distressed. That's very good, Heidi. Pastor Flores told you all that?" Abilene asked.

Heidi found it interesting that Abilene called Diego by his formal name, as though they were in church on Sunday morning. "He just told me the verse. God is gracious to show us what it means."

"God is good, indeed. He's taking care of your brother, Heidi. No worries, remember?"

Still, Heidi wanted to call Ming again. Truth be told, she suspected he had either turned off his cell phone or left it somewhere. The last thing he needed was endangerment when his cell went off in the middle of a surveillance.

She had also called Camden umpteen times. No response.

There was no one else to call except Diego. Heidi didn't want to call him in the middle of the night when he had to preach in about eight hours.

"What's Ming up to, anyway?" Abilene asked.

"I have no idea. He didn't say. I wanted to think it's his usual divorce case investigations, but I think this time it's different. Cam is all over it."

"Camden La Salle? That can't be good. He's with the FBI office down in Savannah."

"Yes."

"Who knows what they're up to."

"I don't care. I just want Ming home." Heidi sipped more coffee. The French press was on the coffee table in front of her. On the other edge of the table was Abilene's crushed can of mineral water. She was falling asleep.

Heidi couldn't close her eyes. She stared at her iPhone, wondering whether she should try calling again. What about calling 911 to report a missing person? Well, it hadn't been twenty-four hours yet.

She decided against going panicky.

Not that I'm not already.

"I'll wait another half an hour," she said to Abilene. It was more a note-to-self.

CHAPTER FOURTEEN

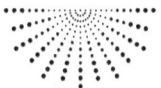

*W*hen she opened her eyes again, it was 4:37 a.m. on her iPhone screen.

She let out a mini shriek. She'd slept for two hours.

The house was all quiet, and Abilene was fast asleep with her mouth open.

"Lord, please let him be home." Heidi half walked and half ran toward Ming's bedroom down the hallway. "I mean here, Lord, on earth, not our final home in heaven. Not that home, not yet."

The bed wasn't made, and there was no one in it. Heidi checked the bathroom. No one there either.

Maybe he's just late.

Almost five hours late. Okay. That could happen.

"Lord, where is my brother?" Heidi looked upward.

She wondered what time Diego woke up. It was Sunday now. Church day. Sunday School started at nine o'clock, and the church service started at eleven. She wondered when Diego usually left for church. She had no idea. All she knew was that Diego was usually the first person there. It was as if he lived upstairs.

Hesitantly, she texted Diego.

Ming hasn't come home yet. Please pray.

She even sounded calm.

She remembered what Diego had preached on a few months before. He had reminded the congregation that whenever they had a crisis, it was wise to call on God first before anyone else.

"Lord, help me. Help us. Help Ming." Heidi padded back to the living room. Abilene was still asleep.

Heidi had a headache now from her lack of sleep and all that stress that came with not knowing where her brother was. She wondered if she'd make it to church this morning. Maybe not Sunday School, but possibly to the church service. The temporary church location in a storefront was about twenty minutes away from here.

Ping!

It was Diego. He had texted back.

Prayed. Don't worry. God protects.

Heidi began praying. "Lord Jesus, I have no idea how to pray about this situation. You know my brother best. You know where he is, what he's doing. I'm worried about him, and I know I shouldn't be. I should keep praying and trusting You to protect Ming. I'm afraid. Psalm something says that whenever I'm afraid, I will trust in You. I'm prepared to trust You, whatever the outcome, but I pray that all is well and that You'll bring Ming back here safely."

She paused.

"I'm sorry I was such a burden to him. I don't want him to work so hard just to make ends meet to support my living in his house. I need to get my stupid dissertation completed so I can be done with school, get a job, and ease my brother's financial load. What do You think, Lord?"

Heidi picked up her coffee mug and French press from the coffee table. She washed them out in the kitchen sink.

She continued to pray as she stood over the sink. She was too numb to weep. She had to get her mind off her brother and onto God, and focus on Him who could protect more than her worry could.

"What if—"

Her iPhone rang. She nearly dropped her coffee

JAN THOMPSON

mug on the floor. She caught it in midair. Her shaking hands placed it on the island counter. She wiped her wet hands on a dish towel.

The phone was still ringing when she reached it. It was Diego.

"Did you get my message?" Diego asked.

"Yes. Thank you for praying and for the reminders." Heidi leaned against the kitchen counter. It felt good to hear Diego's voice. It was calm, soothing, low key. No stress in it at all. It was like therapy sent from God.

That lasted about five seconds. Then: "What if Ming is dead? I'll be all alone!"

"Heidi?"

"Yes?"

"You're never alone. You have God. And you have me."

"You?"

"You'll always have me."

"What do you mean, Diego?" Heidi pressed a hand to her forehead around her eye sockets. She felt another headache coming. She really needed to get in bed and sleep this off. But Diego had said something to her. Something she hadn't expected.

"I'm here, Heidi. That's what I meant."

"You said always. You can't say *always*. You can't always be there. Five years from now when

Riverside Chapel thrives, you'll leave for another church plant. Am I right?"

"Do you want me to stay?"

Why is he asking me?

"What does God tell you to do?" Heidi asked.

"I'm still praying."

"Then wait for God to tell you."

Silence.

"Hello? Are you there?" Heidi looked down at her iPhone. It was still on. She put it back against her ear.

"I'm here," Diego assured her. "I was thinking about what you said. I'm waiting for God, yes. What about you?"

"Me?"

"Are you panicking, or are you waiting for God to bring Ming home safely?"

Heidi cringed. "Both, I think."

"You can't have both. Now I'm going to tell you to do something you might not want to do."

"What?"

"I'm telling you to go to your bedroom and go to sleep."

"But Cam could call."

"I've already texted him to call me before he calls you. I'm going to stay here and watch the phone. I want you to go to bed and get some sleep. Put your phone nearby in case I call. At eleven o'clock I want to see you at church. You might get about five hours of sleep between now and then."

"And you said I was bossy."

"I did not."

"You did too. You called Ming and me bossy."

"Ming said that?"

"Uh-huh. I believe him."

"Maybe it's out of context, but we'll worry about that later. Right now, get some sleep and come to church. Is anyone there with you?"

"Abilene."

"Good. I don't want you to be alone. I'll be praying for you and Ming. I've also called a couple of friends to pray. So we're all prayed up, if you can call it that."

"Thank you."

"Did you get the rest of what I said?"

"Yes, but—"

"I'm awake now. It's my turn to keep vigil, Heidi. Let me take this shift. You need sleep, or you won't be able to process information when we need you to be lucid. Do this for Ming's sake."

"You're very persuasive, Diego."

"Ha. Wish that translated into my personal life."

CHAPTER FIFTEEN

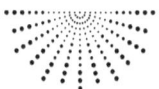

"Want more?" Diego flipped the pancakes on the stainless steel pan. He turned down the burner.

On the counter, half a mixing bowl awaited, pancake mix dripping down the side. He figured he could make maybe three or four more giant pancakes.

"No more. Thanks, Pastor." Nearby, Abilene slid off the barstool at the island and carried her plate to the sink. She rinsed off the maple syrup from the plate and started filling the dishwasher.

"We're not in church. You can call me Diego if you want."

"Brother Diego, you mean? It sounds weird. If you don't mind, I am comfortable with calling you Pastor Flores."

"Okay. Whatever." Diego plated another batch. He wondered whether to make the rest of the pancakes or put the batter in the refrigerator.

He chuckled.

Such a tough decision for a seminary graduate who had helped start two churches in the last five years.

He decided that he wouldn't cook it all. Still, considering the situation, no one might finish what he'd started.

He sprinkled blueberries on top of the last three pancakes. Heidi used to like blueberry pancakes back in college, though he wasn't sure if she still enjoyed them. There had been a four-year gap between the last time he and Heidi had lived in the same town. They had met up a couple of times a year after he went to seminary, but each time he and Heidi had talked less and less with each other.

Their lives had bifurcated until two years ago when their paths crossed again. Ming had called Diego to say that their old church had splintered and disbanded. Ming, Heidi, and some church friends had been looking for a pastor to lead them and grow a new church out of the remnants. Most of the congregation had scattered into other area churches, but Ming and his sister hadn't found an established church that they could identify with.

When Diego's sponsoring churches found out,

they were excited about a new church plant—or replant—and commissioned Diego to go forth.

The mission church in Cozumel that he had wanted to pastor was thriving with its national pastors and didn't need him anymore.

Midtown Chapel in Atlanta already had its own pastor, and Diego didn't see himself being there for years as an understudy to the senior pastor.

Thus, God, in His sovereignty, had moved him on.

Two years later, here I am, making pancakes for my new flock.

He turned off the stove. The clock on the wall ticked a few minutes past nine.

"Should I wake her up?" Abilene dried off her hands with a dish towel.

"I'm wondering whether we should just let her sleep. She didn't get much sleep last night, you said."

"Nope, but knowing Heidi, she'd hate to miss church, especially when you're preaching."

"Well, if she falls asleep in church, what's the point? She can always get the sermons online later." Diego stopped in the middle of picking up the mixing bowl. "I'm not advocating skipping church."

"I know what you mean." Abilene opened and closed drawers until she found a roll of plastic wrap. She handed it to Diego.

Diego cleaned up the side of the mixing bowl with a paper towel, then covered the top with the plastic wrap.

"I didn't bring my church clothes," Abilene confessed. "We left my house in a hurry last night."

"And you need to be in church in fifty minutes to greet people. Why don't you call Nadine and ask her to take your place this morning? That'll give you time to make it by eleven."

"You have to be there too, Pastor Flores."

"Right."

"If you don't care that I wear flip-flops to church, I think I can borrow a dress from Heidi. We're about the same size."

"Great idea, Abilene. As long as you wear shoes, you won't get a cut from the sidewalk."

"I'll go see if I can raid Heidi's closet." Abilene tiptoed off.

Diego made himself a plate of pancakes, leaving enough for Heidi and Ming, should he walk in the door. He heated up some maple syrup, poured a generous helping of it over the pancakes, and sat down to say grace a second time.

Lord, tell me what to do. We can't wait all day for news that doesn't come. Give Heidi strength to endure this, with or without me. You're all she needs.

CHAPTER SIXTEEN

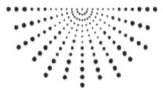

"*H*e what?" Heidi rubbed her eyes.

"He made you blueberry pancakes." Abilene seemed amused as she opened and closed closet doors. "Where do you find handsome men who make you pancakes?"

"My brother makes me pancakes too."

"See what I mean? Winton never did that. No one I've ever dated did anything like that." Abilene was still looking through Heidi's closet. "My brother doesn't cook. If we let him into the kitchen, he would burn down the house."

"What are you doing?" Heidi sat up.

"May I borrow a dress or something to wear to church? I don't think there's enough time for me to get back to my house." Abilene opened another closet door. "Look at all these clothes you have. I never see you wear them."

"I should clean out my closet. Take whatever you want. Well, whatever fits. You're skinnier than I am."

Abilene laughed. "Not anymore, I'm not. I just ate four big pancakes."

"Four? Are you kidding me? You're in trouble, girl."

"I know. I know."

Heidi checked her iPhone. No messages from Cam or anyone else. "Any news about my brother?"

"No. Pastor Flores is on it."

Heidi nodded. "I guess I'd better get ready, in case someone calls."

"Pastor Flores also says we should all go to church this morning. You too, if you can stay awake."

"I plan on it. It'll keep me busy." Heidi opened her Bible. She looked up. "Don't you have to be at church by ten o'clock?"

"Nadine is going to fill in for me as a greeter. Pastor Flores is driving you and me to church."

"Isn't he all things to all people? Chauffeur. Cook. Counselor."

And charmer.

"May I borrow a towel?" Abilene asked.

"Sure thing. There's a stack of clean towels

under the sink in Ming's bathroom," Heidi said. "You're welcome to use his shower. I'm sure he doesn't mind."

"Thanks. I'll need a hair dryer."

"Should be one there in his bathroom. Last door to the right down the hallway."

After Abilene left the room, Heidi opened her Bible to Deuteronomy 31:8 and camped there for a good five or ten minutes as she tried to memorize it.

She prayed before she dragged herself into the bathroom. She placed her iPhone on her vanity after turning up the volume to its full strength. That way she could hear it from the shower.

It was the fastest shower she'd ever taken.

She had worried for nothing. The phone didn't ring.

It didn't ring until she was getting dressed.

"Cam? Cam!" she yelled into her iPhone as she zipped up her church dress. "Where's my brother?"

"Calm down, Heidi."

Heidi took a deep breath.

"I meant to call Diego," Camden La Salle explained. "I'm going to hang up now."

"No, wait. Why do you need to talk to Diego? Talk to me, Cam!"

"I'll let him explain it to you."

"What's happening? Where's Ming?" Heidi

rushed out of her bedroom, barefoot, her hair hanging damp over her shoulders.

She reached the kitchen, motioned to Diego, but he squinted his eyes, as if trying to figure out what she was trying to tell him.

"I'm not going to tell you anything if you don't calm down," Camden continued on the phone. "Let me call Diego first, and then one of us will call you back."

"Diego is right here. Why don't you talk to me, Cam?"

"Wait. What? Diego is with you? Are you at your house? Why is Diego with you at your house?"

Heidi ignored that. She pressed the speakerphone button and placed the iPhone on the kitchen island in front of Diego.

"Hey, Cam." Diego's voice was calm. "What's up?"

"Everything's fine. We're all fine."

"Thank God!" Heidi cupped her face with her hands.

"Diego, I need you to do Heidi a favor," Camden said.

"Anything, man."

"Turn off the speakerphone and talk to me."

"No!" Heidi lunged for her iPhone, but Diego grabbed it first.

"It's okay, Heidi. Give us a minute." Poker-faced, Diego listened on the phone. "Got it, Cam. See you there." He hung up.

"What, Diego?" Heidi took her phone back from him. "What did Cam say?"

"Something happened in the night, and both Ming and Cam were injured."

Heidi cupped her face in her hands.

Diego was immediately at her side. He spoke quietly. "They're at the hospital, and they'll be fine."

"You sure?"

Diego nodded. "No worries, Heidi. Everything will be all right."

No worries.

That was what Ming always said to her.

"I want to talk with Ming," Heidi said.

"Can't. He's in surgery."

"Surgery? So not everything is fine."

"He will be."

Abilene came down the hallway, dressed in one of Heidi's calico dresses. "Ready."

"A slight change of plans," Diego said. He filled Abilene in on what happened.

"First, let's pray." He gathered Heidi to one side of him.

Abilene stood on the other side, holding Heidi's other arm.

"Father God, we come before You now, thanking You that You're the sovereign God of the universe and this world in which we live. We thank You for rescuing my brother in Christ, Ming, my best friend, my buddy, my pal, and sometimes pain in the neck. We ask now for Your continued protection and provision as we go forward. In Jesus' Name I pray. Amen."

"Amen. Diego?" Heidi tried to read his eyes.

"Yes?"

"Will you be honest and truthful with me?"

"Always."

"How extensive are Ming's injuries?"

"Cam didn't say. But first, I need you to pack whatever you need to stay for the rest of the day at the hospital. Bring something to work on. Can you do that?"

"Sure."

"I've been to SMH. Sometimes it's cold in the waiting room. A sweater might help. If you bring a laptop, don't forget the power cable. You have two minutes to get your things."

"I'll be right back." Heidi was off.

CHAPTER SEVENTEEN

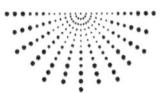

or the first few minutes after they got in the car, Heidi shook badly. Yet to Diego she had never been more beautiful, sitting there on the passenger side of his car, eyes closed, praying silently as he drove her and Abilene to the Savannah Memorial Hospital.

Heidi clutched a straw tote bag on her lap. It had an open top, and Diego had seen some of the contents earlier. A laptop, some clothes, and a Bible. There might be other things inside, but those were the three things he had spotted. He wondered why she hadn't brought her usual backpack, but he didn't want to pry. He guessed that she needed a bigger bag to stuff the sweater in.

The longer she prayed, the calmer she looked to

Diego, until she stopped shaking altogether. She released her grip on the tote bag.

Thank You, Lord, for Your grace toward Heidi.

Diego reached over and held her hand. It was soft and warm and somehow strong, such a contrast to the Heidi before with her shaking fingers and quivering voice. It was as though Heidi was emerging from her cocoon.

She didn't pull away. Instead, she squeezed Diego's hand.

Heidi lifted her head and turned toward him. He kept his eyes straight ahead, preparing himself for whatever Heidi was going to say. He had expected her to break down the moment he told her that they had taken Ming to the Level I Trauma Center at Savannah Memorial.

She did not. *Surprise, surprise.*

Instead, not only did Heidi thank God that Ming was alive, but she found a new resolve.

Wow, Heidi.

Then again, it could be shock.

Diego said nothing. He only felt her hand in his. In the backseat, Abilene was on her iPhone. He could see her in the rearview mirror. Lots of worried faces today, but Heidi had turned a corner.

"The service starts at eleven, Diego," Heidi said quietly.

"Uh-huh."

"It's past ten."

"Uh-huh."

"Are you going to make it?"

"I'm going to drop you off, turn around, and go. It's only ten minutes to church from the hospital. Sunday traffic should be mild."

"I don't want you to miss church."

"If I do for some reason, Roger is going to preach for me."

"Roger? Are you kidding me?" Heidi chuckled. "Dr. Roger Patel, the Sunday School teacher with ten-page handouts for every ten-minute lesson?"

Diego found that amusing. "He's thorough, for sure."

"I know a dissertation when I see one."

"You doubt Roger? He loves the Lord."

"Yes, I agree with that. And he tells the truth as it is. I'm sorry. I should know better. God can use anyone, even a physician, to preach a sermon."

"Even more so. You know that Jesus is our Great Physician. I'm sure there's a lesson out of that that Roger is preparing now."

"Now? Is he going to preach a hit-and-run sermon?"

"He has enough materials. All those Bible studies he has attended and taught over the years will come into play now. This is like the finals for him. He'll be fine."

"I don't know how you remain so calm," Heidi said.

"I wonder about you too. I expected you to completely fall apart."

"I'm learning to trust in God when I'm afraid. Psalm something."

Diego was pleased she had remembered. "Psalm 56:3."

Whenever I am afraid,
I will trust in You.

"Right. And Deuteronomy something. God goes before us. He's with us. He won't fail us. He won't forsake us."

"We need not fear or be dismayed. Heidi, you should preach this morning."

Heidi smiled. "Not my calling. My calling is to support you."

What did she just say?

Diego nearly rammed into the truck in front of him on Oglethorpe Avenue, one block away from the hospital entrance.

~

*V*alet parking at the Savannah Memorial Hospital curb had saved the trio time. They walked down the hallway, took the elevator, zigzagged here and there until they reached the nurses' station outside the surgical rooms. Behind the nurse on duty was an enormous clock hanging on the wall, taunting Diego to flee. He was running out of time, and he knew it.

It was twenty to eleven.

Diego had to leave within five minutes to make it to church before the choir sang. With parking on weekends being a premium, he could still miss the offering.

Lord, please be with Roger. Give him the words to preach this morning in my place.

"He's still in surgery," the nurse said.

Not the words Diego wanted to hear.

"Any idea how long it's going to take?" Heidi asked. Her voice was calm and sure.

Diego was proud of her. What a turning point in her life!

"It could be a while," the nurse replied. "As soon as someone is available, he or she will speak with you about your brother's injuries. Have a seat in the waiting room, ma'am. There's Wi-Fi and vending machines in there. The lunchroom is downstairs."

"Thank you." Heidi picked up her tote bag. "Where's Abilene?"

"Restroom." Diego pointed down a hallway. Then another. He really didn't know where the ladies' room was. *Somewhere.*

"If you leave right now, you'll make it just in time to preach," Heidi said.

"But Roger can—"

"You're the pastor of Riverside Chapel. Do your job."

"I don't want to leave you." There. He said it. He waited for Heidi to react.

"God is with me."

"Yes, He is." Diego didn't move.

He thought he could text Roger to tell him to share his salvation testimony instead of preaching a full sermon. That could buy Diego an extra ten minutes of time.

Heidi was right. He could make it.

But—

He still didn't move from where he was standing.

"Go preach, Diego." Heidi placed a soft palm on his chest. "There is a sermon the congregation needs to hear this morning. Only you can preach it. If you don't go, they will miss the lesson. Then how are you going to answer to God for that?"

Wow, Heidi.

Diego rested his larger hand over hers. Then he lifted her hand and kissed her fingers. What she had said to him in the car meant more now.

My calling is to support you.

Before he could say anything, Abilene returned. Heidi and Diego both dropped their hands.

"You two, go to church." Heidi waved them off.

"You sure you don't want me to stay?" Abilene asked.

"I'm waiting for Ming to get out of surgery. It's a lot of waiting with no new information. I'll work on my dissertation to take my mind off the surgery."

"I'll come back right after church," Diego said.

"Drive safely." Heidi grinned. "We don't want more casualties."

Diego laughed. *That's my Hei—What? She's not mine.*

He couldn't believe what just went through his mind.

CHAPTER EIGHTEEN

*H*eidi was working on her laptop in the waiting room when in walked Camden La Salle, her ex-boyfriend who had never left town.

In every way, he was the man. Muscular, tall, no-nonsense type of guy who accomplished everything he set out to do and then some.

And the man who had broken her heart when he couldn't keep his pants zipped up while on an undercover mission overseas.

The fact that he had felt his confession to her and his rededication to God were reasons enough for her to take him back was the last irony she could handle.

A while ago now...

Camden limped across the fairly large waiting

room and slowly sat down in an armchair next to Heidi. Blood was seeping out of a couple of bandages on his arm. His jeans were dirty and slightly ripped. He smelled like dirt and grime and male sweat. Kind of like how he had smelled when he had been the quarterback of their high school football team.

"Not a word." Camden winced.

"I didn't say anything."

"Shhh." Camden closed his eyes.

Heidi ignored him. She had plenty of things to occupy her mind while she waited for her brother to come out of surgery. Her dissertation, for example. It was September. In two months, she had to hand in her final dissertation if she wanted to graduate in December. But first, the draft.

"Have you spoken to the doctor?" Camden didn't turn his head.

"No." Heidi stopped typing. "As you know, Ming is still in surgery."

"I know you're angry at me."

"I'm not, Cam. I'm sad and disappointed."

Camden smiled. That smile used to turn Heidi's legs into jello, but she had grown up since then.

"This should cheer you up," Camden said. "I was fired two hours ago."

"Good."

"I'm under investigation for insubordination."

"Not surprising."

"I'm going to need a job, and I'll be asking Ming to hire me."

"No."

"It's not your company."

True. Heidi had no rebuttal for that.

"In case you're wondering, I didn't influence Ming for the worse. He asked me for the job. I didn't offer it."

Heidi stopped typing again. If this kept going, she'd have to rewrite this entire page. "What job?"

Camden looked furtively around the room. "Can't say much. Needless to say, if we had more people in the team, we might not have both been shot. You should be thankful the three of us made it. Two other team members are dead."

"Oh, that's awful. I'm sorry."

It could've been Ming among the dead.

"Thank you for your sympathy. Can we kiss and make up now?"

"No."

"I thought so. Well, my girlfriend wouldn't like it."

"You have a girlfriend?"

"Don't sound so surprised. Of course I have a girlfriend."

"So where is she?"

"In ICU. Ming and I dragged her out of that

firefight just in time."

"Oh. Is she going to be all right?"

Camden shrugged. "Touch and go, the docs say."

"We'll pray for her. What's her name?"

"Daljeet." Camden stretched his legs. "We should never have—never mind. It'll all be in the report."

"How did Ming get involved?"

"He was bait. The perp had never seen him before. All he had to do was—I can't tell you."

Bait?

"Did you say bait? As in being on the front line? As in being thrown to the lions?" Heidi tried to contain her emotions, but they were about to boil.

They made my brother bait!

"I'm sorry."

"You seem to be all right, Cam. Just a few bruises here and there. Ming, on the other hand, has been in surgery since they brought him in this morning. He could die." Heidi held her breath so she didn't lose it right in front of Camden.

"I know. I said I'm sorry."

Heidi didn't respond.

"That's not enough, is it?" Camden snapped. "You always wanted perfection—"

"I do *not*. I want truth and transparency, Cam. Is that too much to ask?"

CHAPTER NINETEEN

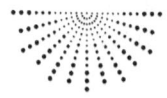

*D*iego wondered whether to let them finish talking or interrupt the conversation. Walking outside the surgery waiting room toward its open door, he had caught the last bits of what Heidi had said.

Truth and transparency.

I can give her that.

With all my heart, I can give her that.

Diego leaned against the painted wall between two framed paintings to gather his thoughts. But he couldn't hear Heidi's and Camden's voices anymore. The conversation was over.

He prayed for godly wisdom.

He stepped into the waiting room. And froze. "Whoa, Cam. You look pretty bad."

"I'm still alive," Camden said as Diego crossed the room to shake his hand.

"That, you are." Diego turned to Heidi. In a gentle voice, he spoke to her. "How are you doing?"

"Okay, I guess. Waiting, waiting." Heidi sighed.

"I stopped at the nurses' station on the way here." Diego sat down on the other side of Heidi. "They think it'll be another few hours before they're done with Ming. I say we go eat lunch. I'm famished. How about you?"

"What about Abilene and Nadine?"

"They've gone to feed Abilene's cat, pick up her car, and they'll be here this afternoon. Abilene is going to stay with you."

"You didn't ask her, did you?" Heidi raised her eyebrows.

"No. She volunteered."

"She doesn't have to. I'm fine. God is with me."

"I know. I'll stay with you for a while, but I have to get back to church for the seven o'clock service."

"I appreciate the company, but I want to take a rain check. We're going to need a lot of help once Ming goes home."

"I'll be there too."

"I know you will, but you also have a congregation to think of, Diego."

"Everything will be fine. God is always good to us."

Heidi nodded.

On the other side of her, Camden snorted. "I wonder if God is really all that good, Diego."

"How can you even say that?" Heidi asked. "He saved your soul. Are you turning Peter on Him?"

"Look at the situation, Heidi. If He is good, then why did He let two of my team members die, and why are Ming and Daljeet seriously injured?"

Heidi wiped a tear from her eye.

"Cam, let's talk about this later." Diego placed a hand on Heidi's.

"No, let's deal with it." Heidi looked at Camden. "Look, dude. God didn't do this. Your flawed, human-inspired, botched operation did this. After you started this mess, we had to run to God to solve the problem, clean it up, fix Ming and your girlfriend. So don't you dare blame God for your mistakes."

To Diego, Heidi said calmly, "Anything to add to that?"

"No, ma'am. That sums it up about man doing his own thing. The lesson is to be discerning enough to differentiate God's will from man's. Many people, Christians included, project one will on another."

"That's too profound for my concussion, Diego. Tell me again later." Camden leaned back.

"We'll pray for you too, Cam. We all need healing."

"Ah, the joy of healing." Camden closed his eyes again.

Joy.

Nehemiah 8:10 came to Diego's mind. That was what he was going to preach on tonight.

> *Then he said to them, "Go your way, eat the fat, drink the sweet, and send portions to those for whom nothing is prepared; for this day is holy to our Lord. Do not sorrow, for the joy of the Lord is your strength."*

"The joy of the Lord is your strength," Diego declared. "Nehemiah 8:10."

"That's a good verse," Heidi said. Sniffled a little. "One of my mother's favorite verses."

"I'm sorry I brought it up."

"No worries, Diego."

Diego leaned toward Heidi. "So. Shall we go for lunch?"

"Might as well." Heidi put her laptop and paperwork back into her tote bag. "You can tell me all about church this morning."

Diego didn't offer to carry the tote bag for her. He knew Heidi. She wanted to carry her own things.

He also knew that Heidi was tougher than

anyone had given her credit for, but the strength didn't come from herself.

It came from God, the Maker of heaven and earth.

"The cafeteria is directly below us," Diego said. "Cam, wanna come?"

"No, thanks. I'm fine. I think I'll take a nap." Camden got up and rolled onto the only empty couch in the waiting room, a faux leather piece that looked super comfortable to Diego.

This afternoon, though, he couldn't take a nap. He'd rather be with Heidi.

"If the nurse or doctor stops by to talk to me while I'm having lunch, please text me," Heidi said. "You have my number?"

"Sure do," Camden replied. "I always have your number."

Diego pretended it didn't matter to him.

CHAPTER TWENTY

"This is not a date even though you paid for my lunch." Heidi placed her brimming tray down on an empty table near a window. The hospital cafeteria was somewhat crowded today with doctors and nurses, staffers and patients, families and friends.

"Agreed. Next time you pay." Diego sat down across from Heidi sooner than she could put her tote bag down on the seat next to hers. "Although we've been saying that on and off since college."

"I like having lunch with you. You always have interesting things to talk about."

Diego didn't respond.

Heidi knew she had set the bar too high. "Relax, Diego. I'm just saying I do miss our college lunches together. Ming was always pulling your leg about your nonexistent girlfriends."

Diego still didn't respond.

Heidi wondered what was up. "Say something, Diego."

"Let's say a blessing." Diego bowed his head and prayed.

Sometimes he asked Heidi or someone else to thank God for the food. Today, he didn't ask her. Heidi didn't mind. She loved to hear Diego pray.

What did I just say?

What would Abilene and Nadine say if they could read her mind? Speaking of whom... "I'd better let Abilene and Nadine know we're in the cafeteria in case they come looking for us."

Diego nodded.

He seemed to be deep in thought.

Heidi texted her friends and told them that Diego was with her. They texted back that since he was, they'd come later when Ming was out of surgery.

Time alone with Diego was probably not a good idea. Then again, the circumstances worked out that way. Or did God orchestrate their circumstances to bring them together? It had been like that for a few months. They had been thrown together in church meetings or the weekly activities they did as friends.

Diego ate quietly.

"What's on your mind?" Heidi asked.

"How life is sometimes."

"Oh, profound. I thought maybe you'd say you like or dislike the way they fried that okra on your plate."

"That too." Diego chuckled. "I do like them a certain way."

"Yep. Not too greasy. Just enough batter."

"You remember."

"College wasn't that long ago, Diego. It has only been five years since I graduated. We met when I was a freshman at UGA, didn't we?" Heidi chewed on a hush puppy. "You were in grad school before you transferred to seminary."

"Nine. We've known each other for nine years." Diego pointed with his fork. "You do like your hush puppies, but you like them better with jalapeños in them."

"Uh-huh. Funny how we both like Southern food."

Silence again.

Heidi dipped a spoon into her vegetable soup. "It's Ming, isn't it?"

"Huh?"

"You're worried about my brother."

"Not worried per se. He could have a long recovery ahead of him. Rest assured, I'll be there for him, whatever he needs. But that'll put you and me together more than ever."

"Is that a bad thing?" Heidi tackled her fried food. Fried catfish, fried hush puppies. Yikes. She decided that she wouldn't eat anything fried the rest of the week.

"People at church might talk."

"About us? There's nothing going on between us." Heidi had started to suspect that Diego was sweet on her, but it seemed he didn't know for sure whether he wanted to explore his feelings.

Yet every time they were together lately, something happened between them. Tuesday, for example. Why had he held her hand and kissed her on her forehead that evening?

Had they moved beyond the platonic relationship they had enjoyed all these years to something more personal?

Diego's eyes were on hers. "Every time I'm with you, near you, I can't—uh, I can't think straight. There, I confessed."

"Wow, Diego. I'm flattered I have such an impact on you."

"You think I'm joking."

"Of course you are. You don't seem to have any trouble preaching at church when I'm sitting at the back of the room."

"Good point. But that's in the house of God."

"As Christians, don't we have the Holy Spirit in our hearts, which technically makes us temples of the living God?" Heidi cut up another piece of catfish. "I don't see you getting all nervous sitting here with me. Has something changed?"

He looked remorseful. Heidi was dying to know where this was going, but she could see Diego closing up. Could it be Tuesday? It was the closest they had been to each other.

"Can we talk about something else?" Diego asked.

"Sure." Heidi eyed Diego's uneaten bowl of okra. "You're not eating your okra."

"Too much batter. Want them?" Diego pushed the small ceramic bowl toward Heidi.

She reached for it, and her fingers touched his. Without any hesitation, he held her hand in his.

He looked up at Heidi. "See what I mean? It just happens."

Heidi loosened her hand from Diego's. She started on the key lime pie. "Want some?"

"No, thanks. I need to cut back on desserts. Lots of church members send me pies."

"That's because they think you're a starving single pastor."

Diego burst out laughing.

Heidi wasn't sure what was so funny.

"Few people know I cook." Diego set aside his tray.

"You're independent."

"Being independent is good." Diego paused. "You know I don't mean being independent from God."

"Being too careful is not, though," Heidi counterpointed.

"You think I'm being too careful?"

Heidi nodded. "That's why you're still single."

"My grandfather didn't get married until he was over forty years old. He preached for many years without a wife by his side. Didn't hurt him any."

"Your dad?"

"Well, he married in college. Went on to have five boys. Now he's retired with nothing to do but drink latte by the sea."

"Are you more like your dad or your grandpa?"

"I don't know. What do you think?"

"I don't see you as someone who'd want to be single for the rest of your life."

"Who knows?"

Heidi polished off the rest of the pie. It was a small slice to begin with. "What about the single ladies at church? Highly eligible. I can name a few—"

"Heidi, the church is not a singles' club."

"But the women are like-minded. Christian, godly, and already in church."

"It's hard for a single pastor to date."

Heidi had to agree with him. "I guess. Some might think your girlfriend is there beside you because of your position."

"Exactly."

"People often look up to pastors, especially handsome, dynamic ones. It's hard to be objective, to separate the pulpit from the person."

Diego put his paper napkin down on his tray. "You think I'm handsome and dynamic."

"Don't let it go to your head. I also think you're one-track, stubborn, and exasperating sometimes. But you do make the best cupcakes in the world."

"If I weren't a pastor, I'd go to cooking school."

"That so?"

"Yep. But the calling to preach is greater than any other calling in my life."

"That so." *Greater than any other calling...*

"Let's get back to the waiting room." Diego pushed back in his chair. "Want some coffee to go?"

"Sure. Thanks."

Diego picked up her tray together with his.

Heidi waited for him to dispose of it. She prayed as she watched him fill two paper cups with coffee. He put just enough cream in hers. He knew exactly what she wanted in her coffee.

Lord, I feel sorry for him that he can't find a genuine girlfriend who'd love him for who he is as a person, not for what he does as a pastor.

When they walked toward the elevator, Diego seemed resigned. It was on his face. In his gestures. In that distant, clinical way he walked beside Heidi, as if they were marching in unison and yet not together in mind and spirit.

Heidi wanted to reach for his hand, to hold it, to tell him he wasn't alone.

However, she didn't. She gave him space, for better or worse.

CHAPTER TWENTY-ONE

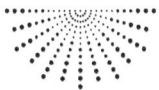

*A*t half past three o'clock, a surgeon came through the double doors and met Heidi and Diego in the waiting room. He introduced himself as Dr. Onada. He went through a long laundry list of internal injuries in Ming that he and his team had repaired. He ended on a positive note about the six-hour series of surgeries.

"Your brother is going to be fine," Dr. Onada said.

Those were the sweetest words Heidi had heard all day. *Praise the Lord!*

She was so happy she gave Diego a bear hug. The man was stiff. She wasn't sure why. Wasn't he happy too that Ming had come through?

"Others have died with fewer injuries than he suffered," Dr. Onada continued. "He's going to have a long recovery process, but he'll live. He's a lucky guy."

"To us, it's not luck, but the Lord." Heidi felt bold enough to say it. "God rescued my brother."

Diego nodded.

"We'll have a couple more minor surgeries tomorrow," Dr. Onada said. "I don't think he needs to stay too long here. He'll be home by this weekend."

"Good. Thank you," Heidi said.

After telling them to stop by the nurses' station to find Ming's recovery room, Dr. Onada left.

Heidi packed up her laptop and tossed all her stuff into her straw tote, sandwiching her laptop in between her sweater and printouts.

"Would you like me to help you carry that?" Diego asked.

"Thank you, but I can manage."

"All right."

That was Diego, Heidi decided. Always literal. He never pushed for more. If she said she didn't need any help, he took her at her word. If she decided she needed help later, it took a while for Diego to understand that things changed.

Things were going to change more with Ming injured. Heidi was ready to care for her only sibling. Whatever it took. She prayed quietly that God would give her strength and time to be Ming's caregiver through his recovery, and to finish her dissertation.

My dissertation.

She asked God to give her wisdom about that. She had planned on graduating in December, but Ming's condition would affect that. Perhaps it made more sense for her to postpone it to the spring. It would be only five months later. Then she could start work in the fall, wherever God led her.

The nurse gave them a printout, and they headed for the elevator. It was slow and full.

"We could take the stairs," Diego suggested.

And so they did.

On the way up three floors, Heidi thought that they had some morsel of privacy in the stairwell. "May I ask you a question?"

"Sure."

"I'm thinking of pushing my graduation to the spring. What do you think?"

"Is it because you think Ming needs you?"

Heidi nodded.

"Why don't we wait and see? After this week, we'll have an idea of how much care Ming needs. Knowing how self-sufficient and independent he is, I wouldn't be surprised if he needs little help."

His voice was distant. Something was off, and Heidi couldn't put her finger on it. "Are we all right?"

"What do you mean?"

"Since our conversation at lunch, you seem to have left the building. Like you're in a cocoon, a bubble."

"I'm thinking about things." Diego's eyes met hers.

"We're best buddies." She nudged his arm. "You can tell me."

"Later, maybe." He opened the fire door and waited for Heidi to walk through with her big tote.

They walked side by side to Ming's recovery room. Diego led the way. Heidi had no problem with that because he had a better sense of direction than she did. To Heidi, all the hallways looked the same.

But she could see other things that Diego couldn't. "If I didn't know any better, I'd say you're unsure about what you want in life."

"You evaluated my entire personal life based on the fact that I was busy thinking between lunch and now?"

"I want you to know that if you want to talk, I'm here. I'm sure Ming would say the same too, if he could."

"Some things I have to deal with on my own."

"You're not on your own, Diego. You have God, and you have us."

Diego seemed to be thinking about that.

"I'm here to support you," Heidi said. "Remember that."

"I do. I think you're one of my strongest supporters at Riverside. I appreciate that."

"I'm also your old friend."

"We're not that old. Don't make us thirty before we get there."

"Don't let Ming hear that. He's turning thirty in December."

"That so? I keep forgetting he's older than I am."

"Yeah. Three years working before going back to college will push you back some."

"Doesn't hurt him."

"Nope. It makes more sense than what I'm doing." Heidi drew a breath. "I've got to graduate."

"I'll pray for you."

"Ming said I can't be in school forever."

"I agree with him. That gives you a good reason to finish your dissertation this semester. Get it over and done with and move on."

Move on? What does he mean? "As in get a job and get a life?"

"Something like that."

"I've been keeping track of job openings. Research and teaching work."

"Where?"

"One right here in Savannah, another in Darien, and one more in Milledgeville."

"Which one has the most prospects?"

"Milledgeville. A big research project around Andersonville Prison. I'll be listed as a contributing author. Plus, I'll be teaching American history at a college there."

"Three hours from here. How often would you come back to Savannah?"

"If Ming doesn't need me, maybe once a quarter or something. I'll have to follow the school year calendar."

"Once a quarter."

"Be happy for me, Diego."

Diego didn't respond. He stopped at the door. "Meanwhile, there's Ming. Let's get him settled, and then we can talk more."

Heidi nodded.

When Diego opened the door, Heidi gasped.

CHAPTER TWENTY-TWO

"*M*ing! Oh, Ming..." Heidi's pained voice broke Diego's heart as she rushed to her brother stretched out on the hospital bed.

A bank of windows brought in the afternoon sunlight, but the rays didn't reach the bed. The room was cold, too cold for Diego, but he didn't want to mess with the thermostat. He stood beside the bed, watching Heidi weep all over Ming. At first, Diego thought that with Ming's face bandaged up, he couldn't talk, but then he saw Ming's jaw moving.

It sounded like "hi," but it could've been the first syllable of "Heidi." Diego knew the two siblings were very close.

"Hey, man. We've been praying for you." Diego

patted Ming's arm. It was bandaged. One of his legs protruded from the sheets. It had a lot of bandages on it as well.

The Feds had used him as bait. He was stabbed in the ribs, shot in the stomach, and left for dead.

Served Camden right for losing his badge. Knowing Ming, he wasn't going to sue the US government, but any other civilian would have.

The rest of Ming was covered up. Diego was thankful Heidi didn't have to see what had happened to his gut and chest. That much, Camden had disclosed to him on the phone this morning.

It was going to take a while before Ming got back on his feet.

Diego decided he'd call Roger later, and between the two of them, they could get Ming's lawn mowed. Maybe Abilene and Nadine could help Heidi clean up the house or whatever she needed done there. They could mobilize Riverside Chapel to rotate meal deliveries for the next couple of months. The Wei family would be taken care of. Diego would make sure of it.

"Don't worry, friend," Diego said. "We're here for you. God is in control."

He said it more for Heidi because he knew Heidi was listening. Or she should be.

Her hands were shaking again as she gently touched her brother, as if to be assured he was still alive. Ming cringed and moaned as if he hurt everywhere. In the end, Heidi just sat there wiping her face with the back of her hand.

Diego looked around for any tissues. He found a box and handed it to Heidi. She muttered something that sounded like "thanks."

Ming's jaw was moving again.

"No need to talk," Diego advised his old friend.

"T-take care."

"Sure will."

Ming's eyelid moved. "H-Heidi."

Take care of Heidi? "I will, Ming. Don't worry."

"Promise?"

"Yes. You have my word." Diego patted Ming's leg. "Rest, okay? You've been through some long surgeries. Abilene and Nadine should be here anytime now. Roger is working, but he'll stop by tomorrow."

Diego wanted Ming to know that he was surrounded by his church family, as Ming didn't have a family of his own in town other than Heidi. It seemed to resonate with Ming, because he nodded.

"Church?" Ming asked.

Diego glanced at his watch. "I don't have to leave until about six thirty. So I have over two hours to spare."

"T-take Heidi...eat."

"We've already eaten lunch," Heidi said. "Don't worry, Ming."

"L-love...sis."

"I love you too, Ming." Heidi adjusted the blanket around Ming's torso and neck.

The sisterly affection warmed Diego's heart. It was something Mom would do for his four brothers and himself, tucking them in at night or when they were sick.

A soft knock on the door preceded more visitors. Abilene and Nadine filed in with a masculine bouquet of flowers. There were vines and some red tropical bird of paradise flower that Mom sometimes arranged in her living room. There were a couple of sunflowers that Mom—

I sure miss her. And Dad too.

This situation with Ming made Diego think of his own family, how his wasn't much different from Heidi's. While Heidi's parents were deceased, Diego's own parents had been gone for months. Then there were contrasts. If he were to end up in the hospital, his parents would fly home and be right there by his bedside.

And so would his brothers and their wives.

Here, Heidi and Ming were alone.

Not really. God was always with them.

Diego hadn't been paying attention to what the three ladies were talking to Ming about. Whatever it was, it made him laugh, and then he was in royal pain.

"Ladies, let's not kill Ming." Diego stopped the ruckus.

As if on cue, a nurse came in to check on Ming. She was cute, and Diego could tell that Ming's eyes were all over her. It was then that Diego was sure Ming was going to make a full recovery.

Unfortunately, Nurse Cute told them that Ming had to rest and only Heidi could stay.

"He...family." Ming pointed to Diego.

"I'm their pastor," Diego explained to the nurse.

"Come back tomorrow then," the nurse said. "He needs to rest before the next surgery in the morning."

"Before we go, would you let us pray?" Diego asked the nurse. "You're welcome to join us."

"No, thanks. I'll come back in a minute." After the nurse left, Diego gathered his flock of friends to pray.

"Father God, thank You for Your mercy and sovereignty. We pray that You will heal Ming's body and make him well. Fully restore him to perfect health. We pray the same for Cam, and his girl-friend in ICU. Please heal them. In Jesus' Name I pray. Amen."

Diego ushered Abilene and Nadine out the

door. He meant to talk to them alone, but Heidi tagged along. He closed the door behind them.

"Nadine, could you organize meals for Heidi and Ming?" Diego swiped his iPad, checking his calendar.

"Sure thing, Pastor Flores." Nadine swiped her iPhone. "Three times a week?"

"Whatever Heidi thinks is best." Diego saw that her eyes were red. He wanted badly to wrap his arms around her, but not in front of Abilene and Nadine. Too public.

"Next week I could go over to your house to do some housekeeping," Abilene said to Heidi.

"You don't have to," Heidi said.

"I want to. I'll just vacuum, fold the laundry if you want me to, and do the dishes. That'll free you up to babysit Ming when he gets discharged."

Everyone laughed.

"He doesn't do sickness well, that's for sure."

Diego agreed with Heidi on that point. "Leave the yard work to Roger and me. I could go over there Saturday, but I'm not sure when Roger is off."

"You don't—"

"I want to, Heidi." Diego texted Roger to ask. Even if Roger couldn't make it, Diego would go. This bit of service would help Ming not to worry about his lawn and flowers, and in turn, Ming's not worrying would help Heidi.

Yep. This is for her.

Diego was quite pleased that his church members knew how to take the initiative when someone needed help. What he had expected them to do, they were doing without his prompting. He had been thinking along the same lines: food, housekeeping, yard work.

"Thank you all for coming." Heidi gave Abilene and Nadine more hugs. Lots of hugs. "I'll keep you posted."

"We'll be back tomorrow to relieve you," Abilene said.

Diego waited for Heidi to say something to him. Before she could, Camden came down the hallway.

"Daljeet died," he said.

"Who?" Abilene and Nadine looked at each other.

"Cam's girlfriend," Diego said, watching Camden head straight for Heidi.

As much as he wanted to minister to his friend and fellow church member, Diego couldn't help watching in disgust as Camden wept into Heidi's hair and neck, his arms and hands all over her waist and back and spine. He wanted to yank him off her, beat him to a pulp, and throw him down the—

Whoa.

He couldn't believe those thoughts had popped into his head.

Forgive me, Lord.

Sure, he knew he was no match for Camden, who had been an Army Ranger at some point before he joined the FBI, but if that man didn't stop crying all over Heidi, Diego knew he had to do something.

Maybe whack Cam over the head with his Bible?

Fortunately for Camden, Diego only had an iPad with him today.

CHAPTER TWENTY-THREE

$\mathcal{T}$he next five days proved to be the busiest days Diego had experienced in the history of Riverside Chapel. Permits, inspections, city approvals, and parking space concerns were only several of the issues Diego faced concerning his new church location.

He relied heavily on the volunteer services of Nadine Saylor, who was a virtual assistant by day. She had to carve some free time out of her own busy schedule to give him all the information he needed. He kept telling her that he was a pastor, not a businessman who knew everything that needed to be signed.

In the end, Diego reluctantly hired an attorney to handle the legal use of Jerome's riverboat for church services and activities. Thank God the lawyer did pro bono work. It did help that he was an occasional visitor to Riverside Chapel, so he was familiar with the church.

By Friday morning, Diego was too mentally exhausted to even think of going over to Ming's house to mow his lawn. He could use the day of rest on Saturday. The Bible talked about taking one day off each week to rest and recover.

Yet he wanted to see Heidi again.

With great reluctance he talked himself out of rescheduling Saturday's yard work at Ming's house.

After all, Roger couldn't make it at the last minute. Diego could ask some of the teens from church to help out, but then he'd have to pay them. He'd already spent a lot of his own pocket money to get the church relocated. He didn't want to dip into savings just for small expenses.

"Volunteers. I need volunteers," Diego said aloud as he parked his car as closely as possible to the riverboat. He hauled the box of cleaning supplies, gloves, rags in buckets, and scrubbers out of the trunk, crossed River Street, walked through the Rousakis Riverfront Plaza, and stepped up the ramp to the riverboat.

He was dropping off the supplies before going to Savannah Memorial Hospital to help Ming check out this afternoon. Tomorrow, some church members would do more cleaning downstairs where the Sunday School classrooms and nursery were going to be. He would be there too, but not until after lunch.

In the morning, he'd head over to Ming's house. He would stay for lunch with Ming and Heidi, then come back here to take over from Nadine.

If all went well, Riverside Chapel would move here this week and hold its first riverboat service on the first Sunday in October.

Next Sunday!

He put down the box in front of the double doors and dug for his keys. Out of the corner of his eye he spotted something sparkly. He spun around.

"Mrs. Fitzgibbons?" Diego wondered how long she'd been standing at the balcony.

"I'm here to help." The forty-something woman with stretched cheeks ambled toward him, tight white capris stretching over broad hips, sequined tank top bursting at the seams.

"That's tomorrow morning, ma'am. Did you sign up with Nadine to volunteer? She's assigning work to everyone." Diego remembered what his father had told him.

Never be alone with a woman who isn't your wife.

What about Heidi? He had been alone with Heidi a few times.

Heidi is different.

Heidi would never misrepresent him or falsely accuse him of wrongdoing. He could trust Heidi.

He sure couldn't trust Mrs. Fitzgibbons.

Diego glanced around him. They were alone on the middle deck of this old riverboat. He pocketed the keys. No way was he going to open the doors. He hoped it wouldn't rain tonight and that nobody would steal cleaning supplies. He decided then to leave the box on the floor outside the locked dining room door.

And flee!

"I called Nadine, and she said you're dropping off supplies. I've come to help."

Diego cleared his throat. "Like I said, Mrs. Fitzgibbons, we're working in teams tomorrow. Did I say tomorrow? I'm afraid you came here for nothing today."

Note to self: tell Nadine never to give out my whereabouts.

Mrs. Fitzgibbons pouted. "I was hoping to talk with you, Pastor Flores. I need some counseling."

"Nadine has my counseling schedule. Call her, and she'll schedule a time for you."

"It's my husband. He's gone a lot."

Diego backed away. "I'm sure Nadine would be more than happy to set up a time for you and your husband to talk with Reverend Jacobs."

"He's not a member of this church."

"No, but he's one of our pastors-on-call. He's retired now and lives out of town, but he can Skype from there. In the summer, he's up here in person."

"Next summer?" She was still strutting toward Diego. "I can't wait that long. I think Gene is having an emotional affair with his coworker. I need spiritual guidance on what to do, Pastor Flores."

"This is not the place to talk about that, Mrs. Fitzgibbons. Excuse me. I have to go. Please call Nadine. Set up an appointment." Diego was at the bottom of the ramp.

"Oh, yes. You wouldn't know a thing about marital problems since you're single. Maybe you need to be educated, Pastor. How in the world are you going to minister to your married church members if you've never been married yourself?"

"As our church grows, we'll be adding assistant pastors, and some of them are married." Diego was practically on the waterfront now. He walked through tourists and locals. The kettledrum band struck up a Caribbean tune.

"Have a good evening, Mrs. Fitzgibbons!" Diego ran across the street, nearly in front of an oncoming taxicab.

He ran to his car, got in, locked it, and shut his eyes. "God, help me."

It would be more than fine with him if the Fitzgibbons family left Riverside Chapel. Then again, wasn't he here to minister? To rescue the lost? Encourage the downtrodden?

Sigh.

Sometimes Diego wondered if he was cut out for pastorship at all. Sermons, he could handle. But people!

And then there's Heidi.

He tapped a quick note on his iPad to make cupcakes tonight. Tomorrow he'd be at two places at the same time. No time to bake.

And Heidi loved his cupcakes.

If Diego weren't a pastor, he would've been a pastry chef...

Would Heidi have treated him differently if he had been a chef instead of a pastor? Would it have been easier for him to start a relationship with her?

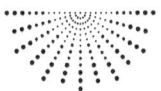

CHAPTER TWENTY-FOUR

"We're almost home," Heidi said to her brother in the backseat of Diego's car.

Ming had groaned all the way from the hospital even though Diego had driven slowly and carefully, not passing the speed limit at all, but keeping a steady pace on US Highway 80 heading toward Tybee Island.

Heidi was happy that traffic was light this Friday. It was way after Labor Day weekend, when the last batch of tourists had packed up and gone home. The locals had gone back to school and back to work.

Heidi chuckled as she remembered Diego's animated story about Mrs. Fitzgibbons Diego had told them back at the hospital. "I'm sorry. It's not funny. It's sad, really."

"Do you realize what I have to put up with as a pastor?" Diego turned south where Highway 80 became Butler Avenue on Tybee Island. Past the library, he slowed down more.

"A *single* pastor."

"I don't think it matters either way. Even married pastors can fall from the pulpit due to indiscretion in their personal lives."

Heidi quieted. Where was Diego going with that statement?

"So the key is to remain pure, right?" Heidi suggested.

"Right. It might mean I never marry."

"Or it might mean you should marry to keep away the groupies."

"Groupies?" Diego parked outside Ming's house. "I don't have groupies."

"Looks like you have one already."

Diego shrugged. "As long as I'm not alone with her, I should be okay. My conscience is clear."

Heidi wondered what he meant. She got out of the car the same time Diego did. They helped Ming into the house. Before they even reached the front door, Ming was begging again.

"I need more painkillers," he said.

"When it's time to take them," Heidi said.

Heidi and Diego helped Ming get into his bed. He said he felt more comfortable lying down. He wanted to be left alone to sleep. No, he didn't want to change into his pajamas. No, he didn't want the curtains drawn. No, he didn't want any soup.

I can't leave my brother.

He needs me.

Heidi closed the door gently, heart heavy and mind burdened. Milledgeville University had replied a couple of days before. They wanted a telephone interview. If all went well, she'd be gone after December. She'd be independent of Ming, and he'd be happy about her not acting like his baby sister anymore.

But would three months be enough for Ming to recover from his internal injuries and be on his feet again?

Did she want the job or not? It would begin in January. It was perfect. She could finish her dissertation in November, graduate in December, and work at a paying job in January.

But Ming...

Heidi sniffled as she walked down the hallway toward the living room and kitchen.

Diego was right behind her. "Heidi."

She didn't reply.

"Heidi." A warm hand touched her shoulder. "Remember what we discussed? 'And the Lord, He is the One who goes before you. He will be with you, He will not leave you nor forsake you; do not fear nor be dismayed.' That verse?"

Heidi nodded. "Deuteronomy 31:8."

"God has brought Ming home alive. Let's trust that He will also heal Ming."

"And Cam too. He's hurting with a loss as well."

"Does he want you back?"

"Who? Cam? Why are you asking me?"

Silence.

"If I didn't know any better, I'd say you don't like Cam much."

More silence.

"Diego, he needs your shepherding as much as any other member of Riverside Chapel."

"He had his hands all over you—scratch that. I take that back. Not my place to comment."

"But it matters to you."

Silence.

"Tell me, Diego." There it went—her hand on his chest again. She couldn't help it. Whenever they were alone, she didn't see Diego as her pastor, but as Diego Flores, the guy she had met in college, who had always kept an eye on her.

Now, she had begun to take note of his attention. Yet his reaction to her interest in him had been confusing.

Diego's hand over hers was warm, as always. He sighed. "You and I—we can't happen."

"Because?"

"I may never marry."

"And yet you go around kissing single women on their foreheads and holding their hands like this?"

"No. Only you."

Only me? "What are you saying?"

Diego let her hand go. "I'm saying it's time for dinner."

He opened the refrigerator.

Heidi peeked in. She saw some prepared food that fellow church members had brought and Abilene had stored for them. There were little notes on the containers with names on them. That way, Heidi could return the containers to their rightful owners. There were enchiladas and casseroles and a big chocolate pie.

"Pie first?" Diego asked.

When she said nothing, Diego put the pie on the small island. He headed for the kitchen sink. He took a long time to wash his hands.

Heidi handed him a dry hand towel. She blocked his way back to the refrigerator. "Will you be honest with me?"

"Always."

"Tell me what's in your heart."

Diego stepped so close to Heidi that she thought he was going to do something. Then he backed away, and the moment was lost.

"All right. I won't ask you anymore," Heidi said.

"If you must know, I can't have both," Diego said. "I can't pastor a church and date someone. I don't seem to be able to do both concurrently."

"Have you tried?"

"It can't work. I want—I can't. If I weren't a pastor—"

"But you are, Diego. How do other pastors handle their love lives and pastor churches too? Your parents, for example?"

"My mom is cut out for the role. She's the perfect complement to Dad."

"If God wants you to marry, He'll provide the right helpmate for you who will understand your calling as a pastor. She will help you and not hinder you. You need not worry. You need not doubt."

"Wow, Heidi."

CHAPTER TWENTY-FIVE

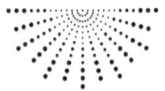

*S*everal weeks had passed since Diego helped Heidi take Ming home from the hospital. Riverside Chapel was now in its new location on the Savannah River, literally, and the congregation was settling into the riverboat on Sundays.

Somehow in the middle of all that, Diego added a new routine of cooking dinner for Ming and Heidi twice a week.

Ming's injuries were healing slowly. His intestines and stomach repaired. He seemed to be recovering some. Heidi juggled caring for Ming, taking him to the doctors, and finishing her dissertation for her second doctorate.

"This is it," Heidi declared as they ate dinner

that Thursday night in mid-October. "I'm so ready to be done with school."

"And yet she's applied to work at a college campus this winter," Ming said.

"I'll get paid to fill in for an instructor on maternity leave, and there's research on the side," Heidi said in her own defense.

"Funny how it goes, isn't it? You don't need your second doctorate after all."

"You mean I could've saved three semesters?" Heidi went around the table to refill everyone's water goblet. When she reached Diego, she smiled. "What do you think? Do you agree with my opinionated brother that I should've left town after my first doctorate?"

"Our paths would not have crossed again if you'd left town before I arrived in Savannah," Diego said.

"Good point. I hadn't thought of that." Heidi reached Ming's side of the table. He didn't want any more water.

Ming's face was etched with pain. Diego felt sorry for him.

"I'll miss you, sis," Ming said.

Heidi sat down. "Not to worry. I'll come home some weekends. It's only three hours away."

"It won't be the same without seeing you every day." Ming turned to Diego. "Don't you agree?"

Diego nodded. *It won't be the same without Heidi.*

At all.

She had made him tea whenever he came over to mow Ming's lawn. She had kept him company when he rested between mowing the lawn and trimming the hedges. She hadn't been much of a person for yard work—he found her too slow—but she supported him any way she could. Hauling away the trimmings to the trash can, raking wherever he told her to, and talking with him about whatever he wanted.

He had been careful not to mention his feelings for her.

Those, he kept under wraps.

After dinner, they threw away all the paper plates and adjourned with coffee to the porch overlooking the Atlantic Ocean. Twilight was cool this time of the year, and a soft breeze blew up from the ocean, dancing around the porch. Diego wondered if Heidi felt cold in her short-sleeved tee shirt and shorts. He didn't ask, but if she was cold, he'd fetch her a woven throw from the living room.

She sat on the deck chair, eyes closed, breathing in the night air swirling above her coffee mug.

Did she want a refill? Diego would get her refills if she wanted. The kitchen door was next to him.

He had no idea how long he'd been staring at

Heidi, but he looked away as soon as her eyelids opened. That was when he realized Ming was squinting at him. Questions were all over his friend's face.

Diego said nothing.

In the distance, a neighbor called out to her cats. Music from another neighbor's house came and went, drowned out by the ocean waves. There were no other sounds. It was yet another normal night on Tybee Island.

Someday Diego might be able to afford to live on the beach like this. He wondered if it was somewhere Heidi might want to live. Or was she here only because her brother lived here?

"Diego."

Such a pretty voice. He loved to hear her voice. Loved to hear her sing. He remembered the teapot song they'd sung with Marie Theroux. He wondered how the elderly couple was doing. He should get back there for a visit, but there had been so many things getting in his way. So many things to do at Riverside Chapel.

Thank You, Lord, that the transition to the riverboat venue has gone well.

"Diego."

Yep, love that voice. I want her by my side as I continue pastoring—

"Diego!"

He snapped at the sharp tone. "Huh?"

Heidi was laughing at the edge of her chair. "Thought we lost you to the night."

"Ha-ha."

"Want to go for a walk? Ming here is going to bed. I drank too much coffee. I need to walk it off."

Ming shuffled in front of them to get to the door. "Don't stay out too late."

"What time is it?" Diego fished for his iPhone.

"Almost nine o'clock. If you want to go home to prepare your sermon for Sunday, that's okay. I'll go by myself. It's a safe zone."

"No way." Diego sat up. "You can't go alone. I'll go with you."

"It'll be a full moon tonight."

"Could've fooled me with the cloud cover." Diego put down his mug.

"Finish your coffee if you want."

"I'll be up all night if I do. Let's go." Diego held out his hand to pull Heidi out of her chair.

They walked across the boardwalk over the dunes toward the ocean. Heidi kept her flip-flops on the entire time. Diego could hear the sound of soles slapping sand. Above them, sure enough, the clouds moved and the moon shone over the Atlantic. The waves shimmered.

Some other couples walked by, holding hands.

"Don't get any ideas," Heidi said as they passed by a pair of huggers.

"Not to worry. We're just walking off caffeine."

"Right. A noble cause."

"When do you leave?" Diego asked.

"My draft has passed the committee. Final dissertation is due in November, and then I'm so done. I'll spend Christmas here, pack, and drive out first week of January."

"Do you want any help moving furniture?"

"I'll take any help you can give me, considering my brother is incapacitated. I'll bring a bed and a dresser. A suitcase of clothes. My books. That's all I'm going to take with me. It's only for a semester, you know."

"Then?"

"Then I'll evaluate where I'll go. I'll probably just stay in the state, considering Georgian history is my specialty."

"Are you coming back for the commencement in May?"

"Maybe not. I've been to at least two commencements."

"I missed them both." But he had attended one of Heidi's graduation parties.

"I did invite you."

"Sorry. I wanted to come, but work got in the way."

"Your *church* got in the way?" Heidi stepped around a pile of driftwood.

Diego pointed to a blob on the sand in front of them. "Watch out. That could be jellyfish."

"Yikes." Heidi walked around it. "Good thing I'm wearing flip-flops."

They passed a couple necking. Diego quickly averted his eyes.

Heidi seemed to find that amusing.

"What?" Diego asked.

"I'd never peg you as shy."

"I'm not shy," Diego protested.

"Uh-huh. You don't go out much."

"I'm too busy."

"Too busy for love?"

Diego didn't know how to answer that.

"You know that God is love," Heidi said. "We love because He first loved us."

"Two verses. You do know your Bible, Heidi."

"Of all the people in the world, Christians ought to know what true love is. The world's love is fleeting, temporal, shortsighted. God's love is intense, forever, and keeps on rejuvenating."

Wow, Heidi.

Right then and there, Diego wanted to ask Heidi to marry him.

But he couldn't.

He couldn't have her.

He'd have to sacrifice something. He wasn't willing to sacrifice anything he had. Not his calling. Not the church. Not his ministry. Not anything. Not for—

But this is Heidi.

"You remember what I said, Diego?"

"You said many things."

"Last month, at the hospital. We had a couple of conversations about pastors and marriages."

"That. Yeah, I remember what you said."

"If God wants you to marry, He'll provide for you."

"She will help me and not hinder me."

"Glad you remember."

"Why, Heidi? Why are you reminding me of it?" *When I'm resisting holding you?*

"Because I want you to know that I'm praying for you that God will bring into your life the perfect wife for you who will walk alongside you in your ministry and calling. I want you to be happy, Diego."

Wow, Heidi.

Selfless Heidi.

"I'll keep praying for you even if I'm in Milledgeville. Come see me sometime, with your wife."

Diego coughed.

I don't want someone else.

Instinctively, he reached for Heidi's hand. Called her name.

"Yes?" Heidi stopped walking.

Around them, the sounds of the surf ebbed away.

Diego was speechless. The man who could preach a mile a minute had no words.

Do we need words?

Diego pulled Heidi gently toward him.

"What's happening?" Heidi asked.

"I'm not sure."

Heidi's arms wrapped around Diego's firm waist. Thanks to all the yard work he'd done, Diego felt happy about his taut abdominal muscles.

"What are we doing?" Heidi asked.

"Not sure."

"You said that earlier."

Diego nuzzled her hair. Pressed his lips on her forehead.

"Don't miss."

"I won't." He kept his eyes open as he tasted her lips. Coffee and cream. Like his. "Surprised?"

"Not really."

"No?" He leaned toward her ear. "I love you."

"Now that's a surprise."

"Is it? I've loved you for over five years. Do you remember when we parted ways?"

"It was a cookout at your house. You were going

to seminary, saying goodbye to your friends. And you made cupcakes."

"I was interested in you, but I had to go away."

"You had to answer the call of God."

"Even now, I have to fulfill my calling." Diego held her. "I love you, but I cannot marry you."

Heidi tensed in his arms.

"I may never marry at all," Diego explained.

"What if I get married to someone else? You can't love me then. That's coveting, right? God wouldn't like that. He sees your heart."

"I don't want you to marry anyone else, especially Cam."

Heidi laughed. "You make no sense. Someday I want to marry and have children."

"I need more time to think about this."

"You want me to wait for you. How long do I wait? Another five years? Ten? Twenty? I'll be forty-seven in twenty years."

Diego had no answer.

CHAPTER TWENTY-SIX

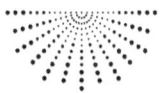

"It's not like I'm going away forever," Heidi said as she sprinkled dressing on her dark-green salad. She tried not to look at Abilene and Nadine. They were still in tears. "Milledgeville is only three hours away. You're welcome to visit me anytime."

"It's not the same," Abilene said. Nadine nodded.

"No, but life goes on." Heidi had told herself that for five weeks since that evening walk with Diego.

He had hurt her feelings badly, but there was nothing she could do about it. She had blocked him out and focused intensely on her dissertation.

It helped that several church members had offered to drive Ming to and from the hospital for his doctor visits and outpatient surgeries, freeing her up to attend her classes at the University of Coastal Georgia, and to finish her dissertation and submit for a formal check two weeks before it was due.

It didn't help that she had found out Diego was the one who had organized the chauffeuring service to bring her relief so she could get her school done.

All that and neither had said a word to each other the entire time. Diego kept doing things for her and Ming, but only while she was in class on campus or out of the house. Since that October night, he hadn't shown up at the house when she was at home.

And he had let Roger take over the senior citizen visitations so that he could focus on settling Riverside Chapel into its new venue on the riverboat. Twice, Heidi had visited Melvin and Marie Theroux, the elderly couple with the teapot song request, but both times Diego wasn't there.

What a complex man! He loved her and had done all these things for her, but he didn't love her enough to care about what they could do together for the Lord.

He had given her the impression that he wanted her, and yet he didn't want her enough to spend the rest of his life with her.

Make up your mind, Diego!

"Are you moving away because of Pastor

Flores?" Nadine asked, dumping an enormous amount of sugar into her tea.

"I'm just stepping out of my brother's shadow," Heidi said.

"So you're moving away because it's time to grow up?" Nadine laughed so loudly that the other customers in Piper's Place turned their heads toward their window booth.

"I think it's more interesting if it's because of our pastor," Abilene said.

"There's nothing going on between Diego and me," Heidi protested.

"Uh-huh. So explain why he's been in a very bad mood and snappy with us at our church meetings? His sermons the last month have been dark and grim. Whatever happened to his happy sermons?"

"It's the series he's preaching. Heaven and hell are serious matters." Heidi could tell that Abilene didn't buy that. Sitting next to her, Nadine didn't look like she believed Heidi's explanation either.

"And what about Sunday after church?" Nadine asked. "He passed by you but didn't say a word. He has never done that. He always sought you out."

"We were in a hurry."

"Stop, Heidi."

"What?"

"You're always making excuses for Pastor Flores. He should know better."

"You can't say that, Nadine. He's our pastor."

"Doesn't mean he's not a human. He's a man in love and doesn't know what to do about it."

Piper stopped by to talk to them. She signed to Heidi. "I have a surprise for you."

Before Heidi could ask what it was, two of Piper's servers showed up with cupcakes! Heidi could eat cupcakes all day long, especially if—

Oh.

Especially if Diego made them.

Heidi didn't let it show. She smiled as Piper signed again. "Congratulations! You finished your dissertation!"

"Thank you." Heidi stood up and gave Piper a hug.

"A few more weeks after Thanksgiving, and you're done?" Piper signed.

Heidi nodded. Signed back. "I have a new job too."

"Happy for you."

"Thank you. Come sit with us and have a cupcake," Heidi signed as she slid back into the booth. She patted the bench.

Piper sat down.

"German chocolate cupcakes!" Heidi licked her

lips. Signed again. "You've outdone yourself this time, Piper!"

Diego would love this—

Sigh.

Heidi closed her eyes.

Lord, help me to let him go. Help me move on. If we're not meant to be, then let me forget him. I pray for forgetfulness.

Somehow, Heidi didn't think God would answer the last part of her prayer. It would take her a lifetime to forget Diego.

CHAPTER TWENTY-SEVEN

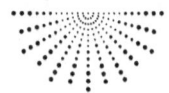

*T*he week before Thanksgiving, Heidi finished submitting the final corrections of her dissertation. It was over. She had marked the calendar for a mid-December graduation. This time, she did not invite Diego. He was the only one she didn't invite. There was no point, really. Their nonexistent relationship was over before it could even begin.

Diego had sent out feelers. Touching and kissing to test the waters. Staring at her like a lovelorn college kid.

Now she knew he was married to the pulpit.

She didn't want to be a preacher's widow.

Heidi opened the closet door. Inside several boxes stacked up from her last move to her brother's beach house. "There. All my earthly belongings."

Ming had said she could leave them there since she would be back in the summer. It seemed to her that Ming thought she might try to stay in Savannah, find a job at the Coastal Georgia Historical Society or even at her alma mater.

On the closet shelf above the hangers, Heidi found an old photo album. She sat on her bed and wept as she flipped through the pages of her childhood days with Mom and Dad, now in heaven.

How could they have left us so soon?

A knock on the door startled her.

"Heidi?" It was Ming.

Heidi quickly wiped her eyes and sat straight up. "Come in."

"Hey..." Ming's eyes were on the album in Heidi's hands. He sat down next to her on the bed. "What's going on?"

"I can't leave you."

"I'm not a big baby. I can take care of myself."

"Ha. That's debatable." Heidi grinned. "Who's going to do your laundry and wash the dishes while I'm gone?"

"I will."

"Sure. You'll be using paper plates until I get home."

"Possibly. Then again, I could do it myself. You've done so much for me that I've gotten lazy."

"That right?" Heidi raised her eyebrows. "What are you going to do while I'm gone?"

"I'm thinking of selling my company to Hu Private Investigations."

"Oh, that's a big one." Heidi had heard of it. Helen Hu was famous in the recovery of historical artifacts. In fact, she had recently recovered a 1698 Stradivarius for its owner, who lived on St. Simon's Island, an hour south of Savannah. It was all over the news. "How did they know about your company?"

"Cam has worked with Helen before. He doesn't anymore since the FBI fired him."

"Poor Cam."

"Don't feel sorry for him. He dug his own pit and fell into it."

"That sounds almost biblical."

"I heard it in one of Diego's sermons," Ming said.

Diego again. Heidi tried not to react.

"If Helen likes what I bring to the table, they might buy my company. I'll go work for them. No more worries about paychecks and healthcare."

"But you won't be able to make the final calls. No veto power when you work for someone else," Heidi reminded him.

"Yes, that too. Something to think about."

"Something to *pray* about."

Ming got off the bed. "Or I can do something else. A second career. I don't mind."

"I haven't even started my first career."

"That's because you never left the nest."

"Did you just insult me?" Heidi scrunched up her nose. "No dessert for you!"

They turned serious again as Heidi began to sniffle.

"As soon as I'm able, I'll visit you in Milledgeville." Ming handed Heidi a tissue from a box on the table next to her twin bed. "It's going to be okay."

"We'll keep saying that until reality sinks in."

They sat there in silence for a while.

"Did you say goodbye to Diego?" Ming asked.

"Diego?"

"Yes, didn't I say Diego? He's been looking miserable. Seems to me you two have been avoiding each other."

"He has been avoiding me. He made sure to do the yard work when I'm not around."

"I noticed that. But you know what they say. It takes two hands to clap."

"It only takes one hand to slap." Heidi slid off the bed with the old album. She put it back in the closet and closed the door. She'd pack her stuff later. It was too painful.

"He slapped you? I mean, figuratively?"

"I can't talk about it." Heidi meant it. She didn't want Ming to think unkindly of Diego. "He's still the pastor of our church."

"I don't care if he's the pastor of our church. If he hurt you—"

"No, he didn't." *Yes, he did. Hurt my feelings and all.*

"I can tell when you're fibbing, sis. You can talk to me."

"I don't want you to beat up Diego or make us leave Riverside. I like it here. This will always be my home church."

"Still...I need to know."

"You don't, Ming. Not now. When I'm ready to talk, you can grill me a salmon burger, and I'll tell you all about Diego and me."

"Promise?"

"Promise."

CHAPTER TWENTY-EIGHT

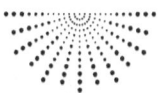

*D*iego had never been more miserable in his entire life. Sleepless nights over the last two months had made him impatient with church members and irritable with his own decisions.

In the last few days, he had begun to question his own calling as the pastor of Riverside Chapel. Perhaps he wasn't cut out for this. Perhaps the best thing for him was to find a church where he could assist. Playing second fiddle to a senior pastor seemed safer than being the man in charge.

Two o'clock in the morning the night after another lackluster Sunday of preaching grim sermons was probably the wrong time to evaluate his entire career as a pastor.

He tried to pray, but the words wouldn't come.

It was as if God wasn't listening to him. How could He? He had wronged Heidi. He knew that, but how? He couldn't figure out that part.

Something was amiss.

Well, anyone could tell him that. As a pastor, surely he had a solution? God would have given him a solution, right? For the last two months, he had searched the Scriptures, rereading all the epistles for a word from God for his misery.

Zip. Nada. No answer from God.

If this were His chastisement for his failure as a pastor, it was painful indeed.

"But, Lord, I sacrificed for You," Diego said aloud from his study. The larger bedroom in his apartment was supposed to be the master bedroom, but he had decided to put an office desk in here and a wall of bookshelves. He slept in the smaller guest bedroom, where a full-size bed took up a majority of the floor space.

It was quiet in the apartment, save for the occasional water-pipe sounds from the apartments surrounding his unit. Someday when he had more income—ha!—he'd buy a house. A real house with land and, possibly, ocean.

He didn't remember the exact moment he speed-dialed Dad. Dad picked up at the first ring. He was at an outdoor café in Sorrento with Mom, sipping latte, he said. Two blocks from their rental flat. But he always had a few minutes for his youngest son.

"God prefers obedience rather than sacrifice, Son," Dad said. "Look up I Samuel 15:22. Read it to me."

"Now?"

"Now, Son."

Diego put Dad on speakerphone and swiped his iPad.

> So Samuel said:
>
> *"Has the Lord as great delight in burnt offerings and sacrifices,*
>
> *As in obeying the voice of the Lord?*
> *Behold, to obey is better than sacrifice,*
> *And to heed than the fat of rams."*

"What does that say to you?" Dad's voice deepened on the phone.

"To obey is better than sacrifice."

"What have you sacrificed? Better yet, whom have you sacrificed?"

Ouch.

"I sacrificed Heidi."

"A pastor sometimes projects an image of knowing more than his congregation." Dad's voice filled Diego's home office. "Who wants to spend Sunday mornings listening to an idiot?"

"You've lost me, Dad." Diego paced the floor. He walked to the window and looked out. There was a parking lot four floors down where he'd parked his car. He wished he had a view of the ocean. But this was all he could afford.

"Let me put it plainly to you. In the first year your mom and I were married, I had just gotten out of the seminary..."

Uh-oh. And I thought he only had a few minutes to spare.

"I was pastoring this tiny church outside Houston. This was before all of you were born, before we moved to Irvine. Your mom was pregnant with Hunter. She was as happy as could be, but there was trouble in our marriage."

"Trouble? You never talked about that, Dad. You two are inseparable."

"Now. But back then, there was a barrier between us at home. I was proud in front of her, condescending, so full of myself. I didn't take off my pastoral hat when I was with her. No, sir. I was behaving like she was beneath me, when, truth be told, we were both equal at the foot of the cross. As a pastor's wife, she is no less important than I am, and I am no more important than she is. Do you understand?"

"How does that apply to me?"

"Expectations, Son. I wanted your mom to think

I'm Pastor Perfect. Truth is, if she cracked the shell, I was a shivering, scared little boy inside. Scared to death of pastoring a church of any size. Most importantly, I was scared to death of being my wife's pastor."

My wife's pastor.

"I didn't want to fail in front of my pretty wife. For a couple of years, my sermons suffered. I preached nothing substantial. Nothing life changing. Until I got right with God, and looked at things the way He did, I wasn't ever going to succeed."

"Am I not right with God? I obeyed His calling."

"His call to pastorship is only one call. He has other callings for you as well. For example, do you think He has called you to be a bachelor the rest of your life or to be a husband and father?"

"I don't know."

"See, that's the problem, Son. Pray and ask God to clarify your purpose. Once you have it, all things will become clear."

"I know what my *purpose* is. I'm called to pastor a church, preach the Gospel, encourage believers."

"After what?"

"What do you mean? After... Oh, I see. Yes, after I love God with all my heart."

"And?"

"And what?"

"To find out the question and the answer, read

Genesis 2:18–25. Then call me back. We're going to Venice for Thanksgiving. We'll be back Friday or Saturday. Call me next week and we'll talk."

"Dad, did you just give me homework?"

Dad chuckled. "My breakfast has just arrived. The love of my life and I are going to say grace and then we'll eat. After that we're going back to our flat to smooch—what, honey? Oh yes, and pack for our trip too. After we smooch."

Diego rolled his eyes.

On the speakerphone Diego could hear Mom laugh at something Dad was saying to her that Diego dared not repeat.

Is this what fifty-plus years of married life sounds like?

After Dad hung up to spend time with giggling Mom, Diego read Genesis 2 on his iPad. The chapter was familiar to him, but since he had been pastoring Riverside Chapel, it hadn't come up much, because he was a single man. What did he know about Adam's wife? Someday he might get to that sort of sermon. Until then, he stuck to preaching what he could testify himself.

He didn't move past Genesis 2:18.

He stared at the verse with its old-English grammar.

And the Lord God said, "It is not good that man should be alone; I will make him a helper comparable to him."

He jotted down some notes. "God doesn't want me to be alone."

He searched his concordances to compare and contrast the verse with the other translations. The King James Version used the phrase "help meet" to mean "helpmate" or "helper."

Supporter?

"Okay. Here we go. God doesn't want me to be alone. He has provided a helpmate for me."

Heidi's words came to Diego's mind.

My calling is to support you.

He blinked. "I have turned away the one whom You have given to me, Lord."

He read on. Genesis 2:19–25 made him feel worse. He reread the twenty-fourth verse aloud.

Therefore a man shall leave his father and mother and be joined to his wife, and they shall become one flesh.

Diego put down his iPad.

He felt alone.

So alone.

CHAPTER TWENTY-NINE

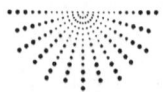

*H*eidi didn't want to be early for church, and didn't want to sit in front where she might make Diego uncomfortable at the podium. However, Piper Peyton wanted to experience the "full church" and insisted on attending Sunday School, which was held prior to the church service.

After Sunday School, they climbed up the stairs to the top-deck dining room where Riverside Chapel services were held. Heidi discovered, to her consternation, that Ming had saved a table ten feet from the podium.

Heidi reminded herself to be grateful for blessings such as Piper, who'd not only shown up at Riverside for the first time in the church's young history, but had also brought several of her friends and a couple of the employees of Piper's Place.

I have to give of myself and not be selfish.

Of course, it isn't convenient to be this close to Diego. But God's work must go on.

Heidi had her hearing-impaired friends sit facing the podium. She placed her chair facing them and slightly to the side so that she could see Diego somewhat but not directly. As she was putting her Bible down, Piper asked her where the restroom was.

"I'll take you," Heidi signed back.

On the way out, she bumped into Diego.

"I'm glad you're here, Piper. Love your café," Diego said. Heidi interpreted for him.

"Heidi has been asking me for many months to come to your church," Piper signed for Heidi to interpret. "I brought friends."

"Welcome to our church." Diego turned to Heidi. "I gather you'll be interpreting my sermon."

Heidi nodded.

"Will you promise to be accurate?" Diego asked.

"I'll do my best. Will you promise to slow down?"

Diego grinned. He whispered in Heidi's ear, "For you, anything."

Fifteen minutes later, back at their seats, the piano started playing.

"This is 'Complete in Thee,'" Heidi signed to Piper and her friends. "First written by Aaron Wolfe in the nineteenth century, it has been put to song multiple times. Ben Nyce arranged this latest tune."

When everyone stood up to sing from the hymnals, Heidi signed the words by heart. She knew all the hymns they sang that morning, from "I Run to Christ" to "His Robes for Mine" to "Amazing Grace," the last of which brought tears to her eyes as she remembered singing it with Diego for Marie Theroux. She made a mental note to visit her again or at least call and see how she was doing.

When Diego went up to preach, Heidi prayed for grace and mercy to accurately interpret the words, meanings, and nuances of Diego's sermon. She asked God to infuse Diego with some sunshine so he wouldn't keep on with his grim sermons of late. And yet, she asked God for only His perfect will, not her own personal selfish wishes to reach Piper through happy sermons.

She wasn't Piper's salvation.

Jesus Christ was the only one who could save Piper and her unsaved friends.

Heidi knew that. She reminded herself to step back and let God have His way.

"Some of you have been complaining that my sermons have been dark the last month." Diego put down his Bible on the lectern. "Well, the Christian life is not always happy days. While we have joy in our heart through salvation in Jesus Christ, we have to face tough situations in life. That's why we need grim sermons."

Diego went on to talk about Ming's long recovery from his work-related injuries, saying that he had permission from Ming to use his surgeries as examples of how God delivered His people from difficult situations.

Heidi remained stoic throughout it, never meeting Diego's eyes. She was grateful that Diego didn't mention her by name, though she was closest to her brother. Diego knew she didn't like him parading her name in his sermons. He knew and he remembered.

"Today, though, since it's the Sunday after Thanksgiving, I'm going to talk about having a thankful heart. Please turn with me to Colossians 3." Diego waited, as if for Heidi to translate and for Piper and her friends to find the chapter in their online Bibles.

Even if they didn't, Heidi knew the verses would be displayed on the screen on the wall behind Diego.

"Read Colossians 3:15 with me.

And let the peace of God rule in your hearts, to which also you were called in one body; and be thankful.

Word by word, phrase by phrase, Diego broke down the verse into points and counterpoints.

Carefully and clearly, Heidi translated Diego's alliterated points into American Sign Language. She was tense in the beginning, but after some minutes, she eased into Diego's rhythm. Heidi hadn't missed a single sermon that he had preached, not even when she was sick with a bad flu a year before. She had listened to his sermon on the web from home even that Sunday.

Yet this was the first time she had to translate it live. It was a bit different from a recorded sermon that had been edited and packaged, not that Riverside Chapel's media team had done much. Diego preached what he wanted to preach, and that was the way it went.

True to his word, Diego had slowed down some. Heidi would thank him later. For now, she'd better not miss his points.

"What is this peace that rules in my heart? More accurately, who is this peace who rules in my heart?" Diego stood at the edge of the podium. "Some of you already know the answer. Jesus Christ, my Lord and Savior, is the peace in my heart. He is the reason Ming can be thankful regardless of his circumstances. Yes, Jesus is the reason I can be thankful. You can be thankful."

When the sermon was over, Heidi was confident that she had done her best. A nod from Diego made her day, though she was sure he had no idea what she had signed.

"Thank you." Piper packed her purse, stuffing the morning program into it.

"Thank you for coming," Heidi signed. "We'll see you at your place. I'm carpooling with my brother, so I have to find him."

"One question before you go."

"Sure. Anything."

"What is this peace that Pastor Flores talked about? I want it in my heart."

Heidi almost couldn't speak. She prayed quickly, gathered her thoughts, and told Piper what she knew. "When I trusted Jesus Christ as my personal Lord and Savior, He lives in my heart henceforth and becomes my peace."

"Savior? What am I being saved from?"

"Sin. We have all sinned and fallen short of the glory of God. Even a single lie in our thoughts can prevent us from getting into heaven. Sin in our heart gives us no peace. It only results in death. However, Jesus died on the cross for us to pay that penalty, so we are absolved in Him. And in Him, I now have perfect peace. Like Diego—Pastor Flores—said, no matter what happens to me, I have peace."

"I want this peace. I want Jesus."

"Would you like to invite Jesus into your heart?" Heidi asked.

"Yes."

So Heidi led Piper to pray and ask the Lord Jesus Christ into her heart.

Afterward, the two tearful friends hugged. "We can start reading the Bible together, if you like."

"Yes. Let's make a time," Piper signed back. "Email me, and we can see what a good time is to meet. How often?"

"Weekly would be fine." Heidi put her hands down. Her eyes roamed the room. "Let's see if Diego is still here so you can tell him the good news."

There he was, talking with a deacon. Heidi led Piper to Diego.

Heidi watched as Diego's eyes lit up more and more while he was talking with Piper about the Christian life, and after he prayed for her to grow as a Christian. Heidi was so nervous she could barely translate all his words into sign language.

The sight was still etched in Heidi's mind an hour later when she ate Sunday lunch at Piper's Place. Diego didn't go with the group of friends, but the life of the party—new life!—was Piper Peyton, who had met her Lord and Savior this Thanksgiving weekend.

It warmed Heidi's heart to no end.

And she prayed that Diego was just as encouraged.

~

"*E*ven the deacons in those Bible days had wives and children," Dad said.

On Skype, Dad was in his pajamas while sitting on his balcony in Sorrento. Mom was reading a book somewhere in their flat, Diego had learned when he first called them on his phone. He couldn't see her because she wasn't in Dad's laptop camera focus.

"Pop quiz, Son. I'll read you the verse. You tell me the reference."

"Dad, I'm not—"

"Try. Ready? 'For if a man does not know how to rule his own house, how will he take care of the church of God?' Where's that from?"

"That's easy. I Timothy 3:5."

"Good for you. I guess seminary paid off. Whew. For a moment, I thought we had wasted twenty thousand dollars a year for four years."

"Ha-ha." Diego was in tee shirt and shorts. He had come home from church, eaten lunch, and sat down when Dad called. It was eight o'clock in the evening in Sorrento, but Dad couldn't wait for Diego to call him back after their discussion on Monday.

Yes, he had done the homework as asked.

Yes, he had waited to call Dad. He wanted more time to think about Genesis 2 and how it applied to his life as a pastor.

"Do you love her?" Dad asked.

"Yes." Diego was sure of it.

"Does she love you?"

That, he wasn't sure. "I guess she does—did. Maybe."

"You don't know."

"She has never said she loved me."

"Does she show it?"

"What do you mean, Dad?"

"Does she respond to you?"

"Every single time."

"Hmm..." Dad rocked in his glider. It made the screen shake. He stopped. "Find out if she loves you and why."

"We're not talking to each other privately."

"You talk in church, right?"

"We talked twice at church this morning." Diego couldn't get over what Heidi had done at church today, interpreting for Piper and her friends. "She led a visitor to Christ."

"No kidding."

"As far as I know, it was the first person she has ever led to Christ."

"David had his men of valor. You have your woman of valor."

"Well, Heidi would disagree with you, Dad. She prefers to work backstage. She's like that."

"You know a lot about her."

"I want to know her more. I want to spend the rest of my life knowing her. There, I said it."

"All the more important to find out if she loves you because of your position as pastor or because of your personhood. That's your next assignment, Son."

CHAPTER THIRTY

"*I* didn't think they do this anymore." Diego felt flustered. It was clearly a setup. He glared at Roger and then at Ming. They laughed, sloshing eggnogs in their mugs.

"It's fake mistletoe. Nothing to it," Ming finally said. "Go on, Diego. You like a good challenge, don't you?"

"You didn't have this last year, Roger." Diego pointed a finger at Roger Patel, host of the annual Christmas party for Riverside Chapel friends.

"Last year mistletoes were in short supply," Roger said.

"Plastic!" Diego swiped the mistletoe with the tip of his fingers. It stayed put. It seemed that Roger had nailed it to the top of the doorframe.

Standing next to Diego, Heidi backed away slowly.

"Oh no you don't, sis. Stay put." With one hand, Ming stopped Heidi from disappearing into the kitchen. "As much as I hate to see this, wouldn't you rather have Diego stand there than Cam?"

Why did Ming bring up Camden La Salle? Diego spun around to see how Heidi would respond. She played stoic. Said not a word.

There seemed to be a stalemate between Diego and her, and yet she had broken the ice over Thanksgiving by inviting Piper to church and then leading her to Christ. All in one morning.

Still, Dad had said it could be because of her commitment and involvement at Riverside Chapel.

What are your personal thoughts toward me, Heidi?

"Surely you've kissed a girl before," Roger taunted Diego.

Not many.

"Technically, I went through the door first," Diego said. "We didn't walk under the mistletoe together at the exact same time."

"What's the difference of a few seconds?" Roger laughed. Abilene and Nadine had now gathered around Roger to watch the show.

"Go on." Ming lifted his mug in the air. "Don't make my sister wait too long."

"He doesn't have to do this," Heidi said.

Diego knew she was trying to give him an out.

Three months had dug a chasm between him and Heidi. He couldn't believe how busy he had been with Riverside Chapel, how the location and the visibility of the riverboat had drawn more visitors than ever to his Sunday services. Tithing and giving were up.

Church planting had been an excuse to stay away from Heidi. Yet as much as he had tried, Heidi was always on his mind. At every church service, she was there. She never missed unless she was sick. Even in her exhaustion of being Ming's primary caregiver while trying to finish her dissertation, she had still made it to church.

And Nadine had let it slip that Heidi had visited Marie Theroux several times on her own to read the Bible to her.

She was everywhere, volunteering, caring, ministering. There was no avoiding her.

In his heart, he didn't want to.

"Well, here we are," Diego said to Heidi.

"Tell them no, Diego. It's meaningless."

"A meaningless mistletoe kiss." Diego lowered his voice. "But it doesn't have to be."

"You take everything seriously, don't you?"

"Kissing you is serious business."

"We discussed this, Diego. It's a dead end, remember? You said..."

Diego reached for Heidi's chin and gently lowered his lips to hers. She didn't respond until he ran his fingers through her hair. The fragrance of fresh shampoo and soap, a mix of green apples and kiwifruit, wafted into his nose. He deepened his kiss.

When he released Heidi, her eyes were closed, and there was a wisp of smile on her face.

So Diego kissed her again.

~

*D*iego found Heidi in the kitchen putting cupcakes on a tray. There was no one else there. "I'm sorry about the mistletoe."

"We won't think about it anymore. Our friends —some friends!—forced it on us."

"I thought perhaps you enjoyed it as much as I did."

"The moment passed."

Diego didn't think Heidi believed those three words.

He waited, but she offered nothing more.

"I've missed you," Diego said. "It has been awful."

Heidi didn't stop plating the cupcakes. "Keep busy. Then you won't think of me."

"The busier I was, the more I wanted you with me."

"Ah, a paradox."

Diego took the tray from her and placed it on the island. "A minute of your time?"

"Time runs out, you know."

"About what I said that evening."

Heidi waited.

"I talked to my dad. Got some counseling on relationships."

"Good."

"I need time to think."

"You told me that."

"Will you wait for me?" Diego asked, expecting her answer to hurt him something fierce. But he was prepared for it. The mistake was all his. He had asked God to forgive him for his indecisiveness about Heidi.

"You take an awful long time to make decisions, Diego. All these internal debates could take a lifetime to go through, you know."

"But when I do decide on things, I stick to my decisions."

"True." Then Heidi did it again. She placed her warm hand on his chest. "Go preach, Diego. Do what God has called you to do. Then come back. I'll wait for you even if it takes twenty years."

Go preach, Diego.

"Would you sacrifice that much for me?"

"I want to have kids when I marry." Heidi's voice cracked. "In twenty years, I might not be able to have my own."

"Heidi."

"But we could always adopt."

Diego was stunned at Heidi's statement.

"Also, our lives are in God's hands. Have you thought of the possibility that one or both of us might be dead in twenty years? That's a consideration, you know. But I'll wait for you, however long it takes."

"You'll never marry?"

"I won't marry until you decide one way or another."

Wow, Heidi.

"Such a sacrifice is beyond my comprehension," Diego said.

"It doesn't even come close to what Jesus did for me on the cross. Anyway, I'll pray for you. My calling is to support you."

"Support me as a pastor or support me as a person?"

"I think I started having feelings for you before you were ever a pastor. As for your sermons, I think some of them are pretty dull, but that's between you and God."

"What? Did you say my sermons are—"

"My point is that I love you for who you are in Christ, not for what you do for Him."

Wow, Heidi.

Diego kissed her forehead.

"Don't miss." Heidi chuckled.

"I won't." Diego searched her face. "I love you so much. I'm such an idiot. I don't deserve you, Heidi."

She didn't get a chance to respond as Diego claimed her lips again and again until he heard someone's footsteps in the kitchen.

"What are you doing with my sister?" Ming asked in a mocking tone. "I sent her here to get more desserts, and she gets waylaid. Shame on you, Pastor Flores. Shame on you."

CHAPTER THIRTY-ONE

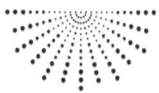

"Thank you, everyone, for coming to church today," Pastor Diego Flores said from his pulpit after the closing prayer. "Hope y'all have a wonderful after-Christmas weekend lunch or whatever you're doing, and oh, by the way, Heidi Wei, will you marry me?"

The congregation roared.

Everyone turned this way and that.

"She's over there," someone said above the noise.

Heidi's eyes grew big. She wanted to slink down in her chair and disappear into the floor. But she froze there, one hand on her Bible, the other hand gripping the table so hard her knuckles were turning white.

Here he comes.

She watched Diego, eyes bright, a silly grin on

his face, walk toward her in what seemed like slow motion.

Before Heidi knew what was happening, Diego was on one knee, a shiny diamond ring between two of his fingers.

So traditional.

"I love you, Heidi, and I'm sorry. I don't want to wait twenty years."

"You put God first."

"It took me five years to realize that God has also called you." Diego held Heidi's hand and rubbed her fingers.

"Yes. To support you."

"How could I not see that? You've been patient with me."

Tears filled Heidi's eyes.

"I don't serve God alone," Diego continued. "Be by my side. Partner with me. Team with me. Marry me?"

"To serve with you?"

"To love me and to let me love you. I want to be with you the rest of my life."

Heidi touched his chin. "Yes, I'll marry you."

The congregation oohed.

Diego rose with Heidi. He leaned down and kissed her forehead.

"Don't miss," Heidi whispered.

"I won't." He kissed her cheek.

And then, in front of everyone at Riverside Chapel, he found her lips.

It was a sweet kiss, but not too long.

This was Diego—who had rarely shown affection in public beyond sterile hugs and handshakes—stepping out, taking one more step of faith, so to speak.

Heidi reminded herself to let him grow as the Lord led. It had to be in God's timing that all these events came to pass.

She had all but given up on Diego. She supposed now she might not stay in Milledgeville past May, when the school year ended. One semester of research wasn't too bad, but for historians, not nearly enough.

Or she might not take the out-of-town job after all.

There were rumblings that the Coastal Georgia Historical Museum was looking to add research historians for the archive library. She might apply for one of those positions.

Driving to Abercorn Street on Savannah every day would be a shorter commute than her six-hour round trip to Milledgeville.

Yes, she'd want to see Diego every day, not only on weekends or once a month.

This was Diego, Heidi reminded herself. She would have to expect long decision-making processes, lingering feelings, and lonely hours when he was busy preparing sermons to preach Sunday after Sunday.

As a historian, she understood the latter part. Her own research and writings took a long time too. Perhaps they could have his and hers home offices. They'd still see each other for lunch and dinner.

At least they could work all day in the same house.

"What are you thinking?" Diego whispered in her ear.

"The rest of it."

"The rest of it? I can tell you this. I'll love you the rest of my life. Only God will I love more. Is that good enough?"

"More than enough."

"That's it!"

"What is it?"

"I was figuring out a title for my next Sunday evening sermon series. I'm going to call it 'More Than Enough.' You're wonderful, Heidi." His lips nearly met hers again, but he stopped midway. "Oh. My mic is still on."

"Sure is, Pastor Flores," Ming said from somewhere in the room. "At some point, you're going to stop kissing my sister and let the church out for lunch. We're starving!"

Everyone broke out laughing.

CHAPTER THIRTY-TWO

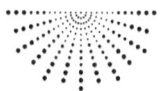

an and wife, not pastor and wife.

Diego chewed on Dad's words as the retired pastor droned on for the benefit of the bride and groom, the wedding party, and everyone else who might be listening both now and in the future.

Still, Diego was glad Dad officiated this solemn ceremony.

His parents had flown home from Italy right after Christmas. After having put Diego and Heidi through an intensive six weeks of marriage counseling, Pastor Samuel Flores declared his youngest son and his fiancée ready for a lifetime of marital bliss.

Well, about time.

So there they all were, in the middle of February

when it was blustery and cold outside but warm enough in the enclosed upper deck of the riverboat.

Diego glanced at lovely Heidi, with her veil lifted and her lips thoroughly kissed, as they waltzed down the aisle in the upper dining room filled to the brim with two hundred clapping and cheering wedding guests.

Some of them were Riverside Chapel church members. Others were local senior citizens to whom the church had ministered.

The rest were family members. The Floreses from Dad's side, the Giordanos from Mom's side, and the Weis and Yangs from Singapore and Canada all mingled and cheered them on.

Outside the dining room, Diego heard the engines purr as the riverboat glided smoothly on the Savannah River beneath the Talmadge Memorial Bridge.

The sun was setting, the sky turning purplish as the day turned into dusk along the Georgia coast.

The air was chilly, but Diego's tuxedo kept out the cold.

"Are you warm enough?" Diego asked his bride as he led her across the moving deck toward the reception room downstairs.

Heidi nodded. "Love this wool wedding gown, but even if it weren't wool, you'd be warm enough for me."

"You can tell me that every winter." Diego tightened his arm around her waist.

Then he sighed. "Do you think Dad could handle preaching the next two Sundays in my place? Maybe we should take a shorter honeymoon."

"We could, if you want. We have a lifetime together. What's one honeymoon?"

Diego knotted his eyebrows. "Are you joking, or are you being serious?"

"No worries, husband," Heidi said. "My father-in-law will do just fine. He has been preaching for longer than you've been alive."

"That's true."

"Besides, we can listen to his sermons live from your parents' flat in Sorrento," Heidi said. "You can keep an ear on him."

Diego stopped Heidi at the stairs.

"What, Diego?" Heidi held on to her bouquet of lilies and roses.

"I can't believe I'm married to you."

"It has only been half an hour." Heidi smiled. "Tell me again in ten years."

"Or fifty. Or seventy." Diego planted a soft kiss on Heidi's forehead.

"Don't miss."

His thumb caressed her lower lip.

"I won't." And he didn't.

DEAR READER:

I hope you enjoyed reading *Know You More*, the story of how Diego and Heidi understand God's will for their lives together. The next book in the series is about Heidi's brother, Ming, whom we have met in both *Ask You Later* and *Know You More*. A romance with a side of suspense, *Tell You Soon* focuses on Ming's life as a private investigator who must sell his beach house to make ends meet. He hires his friend and real estate agent Sabine Hu to put his house on the market. Unfortunately for Sabine, Ming's job puts her life in danger...

Tell You Soon
JanThompson.com/tell

READ A FREE EBOOK!

Set in Georgia, South Carolina, and Tennessee, this Christian romance tells the story of art gallery archivist Sheryl Breckenridge and world-famous sculptor Winton Pace. This book is set in the same story world.

Time for Me (A Vacation Sweethearts Prequel)

JanThompson.com/time-free

JOIN MY BOOK NEWS MAILING LIST

Want to keep up with my writing schedule and get the latest book news from me? Sign up for my mailing list and read my newsletters for behind-the-scene information as well as to get free and discounted books.

Jan Thompson's Mailing List
JanThompson.com/newsletter

PLEASE WRITE A REVIEW

Thank you for reading *Know You More*. If you'd like to leave a review, please follow the link below to see the retailers that carry this ebook.

Know You More
JanThompson.com/know

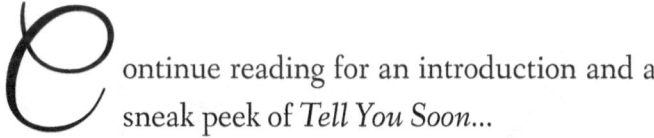 ontinue reading for an introduction and a sneak peek of *Tell You Soon...*

THE NEXT BOOK IS TELL YOU SOON

SAVANNAH SWEETHEARTS BOOK 3

She wants to fix up his beach house and move on.
He wants to fix up her heart and move in.

A private investigator trying to sell his house falls in love with his colleague's sister and gets her into mortal danger.

A Christian beach romance with suspense, *Tell You Soon* is Book 3 in *USA Today* bestselling author Jan Thompson's Savannah Sweethearts series of clean and wholesome, sweet and inspirational, contemporary Christian romances set in the coastal city of Savannah, Georgia, and on the beaches of Tybee Island by the Atlantic Ocean.

SABINE'S SCARS...

Sabine Hu's legs were crushed in an auto accident three years ago, ending her modeling career. Today she walks without a cane, is back in heels, and has found a new job as a real estate agent selling houses in Savannah and on Tybee Island.

She keeps to herself and stays in the background, unlike her high-profile sister, Helen, whose fame as a private investigator is constantly in the news.

MING'S MAYHEM...

Private Investigator Aidan Ming Wei works with Sabine's sister, but he's interested in getting to know Sabine better. He thinks he can draw her out of her shell. Since he has hired Sabine to sell his house by the Atlantic Ocean, he has all sorts of excuses to spend time with her.

She seems to be at ease around him, and they get along well.

However, spending time with her is exactly what would put her life in danger, and Ming risks losing Sabine forever...

Tell You Soon (Savannah Sweethearts Book 3): JanThompson.com/tell

Savannah Sweethearts: JanThompson.com/savannah

To receive publication news about the Savannah Sweethearts series, sign up to be on Jan's mailing list: JanThompson.com/newsletter

Continue reading for a sneak peek of *Tell You Soon*...

TELL YOU SOON CHAPTER 1
SNEAK PEEK

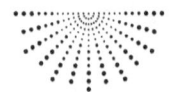

*A*idan Ming Wei couldn't remember how he had been somehow drafted into planning the wedding for his sister, Heidi, to Pastor Diego Flores of Riverside Chapel.

He vaguely remembered that Heidi's best friends had been trying to cut down the costs of hosting a riverboat wedding cruise, and the best way to do that—according to them!—was to avoid hiring a professional wedding planner. The bridesmaids—Abilene, Nadine, and Piper—had divvied up the work among the friends, and somehow Ming had drawn the shortest straw.

They had assigned him to be in charge of invitations.

Invitations!

He remembered telling them: *I'll just send everyone an email.*

And he had done that, much to his friends' chagrin.

Everything had gone well, from the wedding to the reception. After taking the newlyweds to the airport for their three-week honeymoon in Italy, Ming had jumped right back into work with a new client for Savannah River Investigations, Inc.

Unfortunately, he had paid for that mistake by ripping his side again. Four stitches later, he knew his career as a private investigator had ended.

Prematurely.

In the empty kitchen with dusty sun rays shining in, Ming downed some painkillers and dragged himself to the deck.

His smartphone buzzed. A message from Roger, a friend from church, filled the screen. It was long, filled with bullet-points and footnotes, and ended with these words: *Leaving town tomorrow. Pray for my monthlong visit to Mumbai. But tonight, will come over at six with dinner so you won't starve to death.*

Why must everyone baby him?

First his sister, and now one of his best friends?

Sigh.

He turned off his phone and placed it on a window ledge. It was still a bit chilly this late February afternoon, but he was comfortable in his old sweatshirt and shorts.

He climbed into his hammock and grimaced at the pain he still felt in his stomach and side. The internal wounds continued to heal.

Thank God I'm still alive.

He had come a long way since that ambush back in September, but there was a way to go even after half a dozen surgeries. He shouldn't have gone back to work last week, but he had to know whether he could still work.

Well, now I do.

Until he returned to one hundred percent, he couldn't move without gasping for air and experiencing that pain in his side. Injuring old wounds didn't help at all. His being physically unable to do surveillance work killed his business. He could hire someone else to do the work, but he had no money to pay them.

To make it worse, Helen Hu's security firm

hadn't given him a definite answer on whether she wanted to buy his company. He needed an infusion of income, or he couldn't run his business and pay the bills.

Being on disability paychecks shamed him.

Ming prayed for relief. When he looked around, he saw his answer.

His deck railings, the yard with his charcoal grill in it, the fence, the dune, the beach, the waves, and the ocean beyond, all that reminded him that he lived in a much sought-after ocean-front lot.

Taxes and his mortgage were high, and his income was low.

There would be no way for him to stay here, but if he sold it, he could possibly live on the income for a year while he recovered.

He wondered if his sister and Diego would like to buy this house.

Probably not. Diego had said something about wanting a bigger space to hold Bible studies and gatherings.

Ming was thinking about that when he heard a vehicle pull up in his driveway.

The street was quiet this afternoon, as few tourists flocked to Tybee Island in the middle of winter, southern weather notwithstanding.

He didn't think it was Roger bringing him

dinner, because he didn't get off work until five or six in the evening.

Ming couldn't remember if he had locked the front door, and he was sure he should go double-check.

But his body didn't move, and his eyelids were too heavy to open. He wondered who was at the door, but this hammock was too comfortable, and the pain medication he'd just taken was kicking in.

~

*S*abine Hu figured she could list this cute beach house for three hundred thousand dollars.

Sure can. Easily.

It was an older home, but the exterior looked well-maintained and even recently painted. Cheery yellow walls with white shutters would appeal to double-income no-kid couples looking for weekend getaways on Tybee Island.

The bushes on both sides of the front door had been trimmed down to below the windows. The yard was cleaned up and mowed all the way to the curb where she had parked her SUV.

Nice flat lot. Oceanfront. *What's not to love?*

Sabine stepped into the shade of the front door overhang and pressed the doorbell again.

No answer.

She walked toward the front windows. Those white shutters with the heart cutouts were quaint and screamed female. She wondered who lived with Ming.

She peeked in through the windows. Lots of summer light in the cluttered living room with dark furniture and a big television. The living room itself looked like a man cave.

What a contrast with the feminine exterior.

Sabine knew so little about Aidan Ming Wei, only that he was another private investigator like her sister, Helen. Sabine had seen Ming a couple times at Helen's lavish parties she had held in Savannah to celebrate her successes.

That was all.

They had rarely talked to each other. Sabine had generally been busy keeping Mom out of trouble at parties.

Now Helen had given her a padded envelope to deliver to Ming. It had to be delivered today.

If Sabine didn't have four house showings on Tybee today, she would've said no to being her sister's errand girl.

Yet whenever Helen asked for Sabine's help, she was always there.

Sabine didn't know why she did it. Helen had

minions she could have summoned at the wave of her hot-pink fingernails.

But no.

Helen had insisted that this envelope had to be hand-delivered to Ming.

Somehow, after all that the sisters had gone through, she still trusted Sabine more than anyone she employed in her private investigation firm, handed down to Helen by their now deceased dad.

Sabine rang the doorbell for a fourth time. She could hear nothing coming from the house. The only sounds surrounding her were the crashing Atlantic Ocean in the backyard, squawks of seabirds above her, and the occasional vehicle engines from the street behind her. It was only February, and tourists thinned out this time of year. Traffic would pick up by May.

Real estate agents could be patient, but it was pushing six o'clock, she hadn't been home for twelve hours, and all Sabine wanted to do now was deliver the envelope, go home, and sit in her hot tub.

The sooner she took care of this matter for Helen, the better.

Sabine found a stone path in the side yard that led to the back of the house. The hedges between this cottage and the neighbor's sprawl had been cut down to a somewhat boxy look. Traditional.

No weeds on the grass. Good.

She almost stepped on an anthill. Not good.

Sabine rounded the corner. The roar of the ocean was louder past the bushes and hedges and might have muffled the doorbell. She came to a deck of weathered pine, and on the deck, under what looked like a retractable fabric awning, was the man himself.

On a hammock, Ming was fast asleep in a sweatshirt and a pair of shorts with faded yellow paint on them. He was buff and tanned, and his shoulders wide and arms long.

Sabine wondered if he played football in high school or college.

His legs were pretty cut up and bruised. Old scars. New stitches.

Sabine froze.

Old scars.

Old scars were up and down her own legs and thighs too. They were the reason she wore long pants and long skirts when out and about all year long, regardless of how hot it got in coastal Georgia.

And the reason she didn't swim in public any more.

Sabine clutched her purse, the thick envelope inside.

She backed away.

In the hammock, an eye opened. "Sabine?"

Tell You Soon (Savannah Sweethearts Book 3):
JanThompson.com/tell

More Information about Savannah Sweethearts:
JanThompson.com/savannah

To keep up with Jan Thompson and her book news:
JanThompson.com/newsletter

READ A FREE EBOOK IN THE SAME STORY WORLD

Set in Georgia, South Carolina, and Tennessee, this clean and wholesome Christian romance tells the story of art gallery archivist Sheryl Breckenridge and world-famous sculptor Winton Pace. Read this ebook for free!

Time for Me (A Vacation Sweethearts Prequel)

JanThompson.com/time-free

ACKNOWLEDGMENTS

Many thanks to my Georgia Press publishing team for keeping up with my writing schedule.

I appreciate author Heather Day Gilbert for copyediting this book, and copyeditor Dori Harrell and proofreader Lenda Selph for proofreading it. Thank you, ladies!

I am grateful to God for my husband and son for their support and encouragement. I also thank God for my parents and my three brothers for my happy and memorable childhood. I'll always remember my beloved mother and my late father for having instilled in me the love of reading and writing from a very early age. I miss my father here on earth, but I will see him again in heaven someday.

Most of all, I am eternally thankful to my Lord and Savior, Jesus Christ, who died on the cross to save me from my sins and rose again from the grave to

give me eternal life. Without Him, I can write
nothing (John 15:5).

Jan Thompson
John 3:16

BOOKS BY JAN THOMPSON

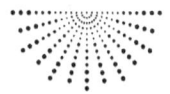

CONTEMPORARY CHRISTIAN CITY,
COASTAL, AND BEACH ROMANCE

Seaside Chapel (7 Books)
JanThompson.com/seaside
Savannah Sweethearts (12 Books)
JanThompson.com/savannah
Vacation Sweethearts (8 Books)
JanThompson.com/vacation

CHRISTIAN ROMANTIC SUSPENSE AND
NEAR-FUTURE TECHNOTHRILLERS

Protector Sweethearts (6 Books)

JanThompson.com/protector
Defender Sweethearts (6 Books)
JanThompson.com/defender
Binary Hackers (4 Books)
JanThompson.com/binary

Subscribe to Jan Thompson's mailing list:
JanThompson.com/newsletter

SEASIDE CHAPEL

Welcome to *USA Today* bestselling author Jan Thompson's Seaside Chapel Christian beach romance series. These novels are set on real-life St. Simon's Island, Georgia—a beach town where history is all around and the future is a moment away—and the neighboring fictitious Seaside Island, where the rich and famous live.

Savor the small-town atmosphere and the warm southern beaches of St. Simon's Island and the idyllic Golden Isles along the Atlantic Ocean. Enjoy the music of the orchestra and hymns of the church, and hang out with our Christian friends who attend Seaside Chapel, a little church by the sea known for its beach weddings and fair share of love and life.

As these Christians grow in their knowledge and understanding of God, they are tested in their

spiritual maturity, their love lives, and their relationships with others. Share their heartaches and healing, and cheer them on as they celebrate faith,
family, and friends.

- Book 0 (Prequel): *His Surprise Proposal*
- Book 1: *His Longing Heart*
- Book 2: *His Wake-Up Call*
- Book 3: *His Morning Kiss*
- Book 4: *His Quiet Serenade*
- Book 5: *His Waiting Love*
- Book 6: *His Beach Retreat*

For more information about Seaside Chapel:
JanThompson.com/seaside

SAVANNAH SWEETHEARTS

Welcome to the new south! From *USA Today* bestselling author Jan Thompson come these clean and wholesome, sweet and inspirational Christian romances set on the romantic beaches of Tybee Island and in the coastal town of Savannah, Georgia. Meet a group of multiracial and multiethnic churchgoing Christians who love the Lord, work hard in their careers, and seek God's will for their love lives. Against a backdrop of ocean, sand, and sun, these inspirational romances showcase aspects of the human need for God and for one another. Have some tea, settle in a comfortable reading chair, and enjoy these sweet celebrations of faith, hope, and love in Jesus Christ.

- Book 1: *Ask You Later* (Artist Romance)

- Book 2: *Know You More* (Multiracial Romance)
- Book 3: *Tell You Soon* (Asian-American Romance with Suspense)
- Book 4: *Draw You Near* (International Romance)
- Book 5: *Cherish You So* (Wheelchair Billionaire Romance)
- Book 6: *Walk You There* (Old-Meets-New Tour Guide Romance)
- Book 7: *Love You Always* (Romance with Suspense)
- Book 8: *Kiss You Now* (Multiracial Romance)
- Book 9: *Find You Again* (Multiracial Romance)
- Book 10: *Wish You Joy* (Christmas-Themed Romance)
- Book 11: *Call You Home* (Deaf Chef Romance)
- Book 12: *Let You Go* (Asian-American Romance with Suspense)

For more information about Savannah Sweethearts:
JanThompson.com/savannah

VACATION SWEETHEARTS

Travel with our friends from Savannah, Georgia, to the coast and to the mountains. Cheer them on as they celebrate the immeasurable grace and undeserved mercy of God through Jesus Christ.

The Vacation Sweethearts novels are a spin-off of Jan's Savannah Sweethearts series, and fans will recognize familiar faces from Riverside Chapel, a church in the coastal city of Savannah, Georgia. In fact, we might even visit the beach town of Tybee Island from time to time to visit old friends and beloved families...

- Book 0 (Prequel): *Time for Me*
- Book 1: *Smile for Me* (International Romance)

- Book 2: *Reach for Me* (Romance with Suspense)
- Book 3: *Wait for Me* (Romance with Suspense)
- Book 4: *Look for Me* (Romance with Suspense)
- Book 5: *Pray for Me* (International Romance)
- Book 6: *Care for Me* (Small Mountain Town Romance)
- Book 7: *Cheer for Me* (International Romance)

Read *Time for Me* (Prequel) for free:
JanThompson.com/time-free

For more information about Vacation Sweethearts:
JanThompson.com/vacation

PROTECTOR SWEETHEARTS

Private investigator Helen Hu and her associates specialize in searching for missing persons and hunting for lost treasures. Join them in their adventure suspense around the world in *USA Today* best-selling author Jan Thompson's Protector Sweethearts, a series of Christian Romantic Suspense with a side of mystery.

Protector Sweethearts is a spin-off of Savannah Sweethearts and Vacation Sweethearts.

- Book 1: *Once a Thief*
- Book 2: *Once a Hero*
- Book 3: *Once a Spy*
- Book 4: *Twice a Fighter*
- Book 5: *Twice a Convict*
- Book 6: *Twice a Soldier*

For more information about Protector Sweethearts:
JanThompson.com/protector

DEFENDER SWEETHEARTS

Defender Sweethearts is a sister series to the Protector Sweethearts Christian romantic suspense collection. While the heroes in Protector Sweethearts search for lost treasures and lost people, the Defender Sweethearts novels focus on protecting the helpless and hopeless. The main characters in Defender Sweethearts come from the supporting cast in Protector Sweethearts.

- Book 1: *Never a Traitor*
- Book 2: *Never a Hostage*
- Book 3: *Never a Fugitive*
- Book 4: *Always a Maverick*
- Book 5: *Always a Champion*
- Book 6: *Always a Guardian*

For more information about Defender Sweethearts:
JanThompson.com/defender

BINARY HACKERS

Like more suspense with your Christian romance? Like to read suspense thrillers? If you're looking for clean near-future romantic suspense without compromising the Christian faith, these books are for you.

From *USA Today* bestselling author Jan Thompson come these inspirational near-future cyberthrillers combining technothriller and romance, starting with Binary Hackers that feature computer specialists living at the edge of cyber-space, where they have to juggle being law-abiding truth-telling Christians while carrying out their assignments by any and all means possible.

The Binary Hackers series is set in the same story world as Jan's other books, and characters from the other series may make cameo appearances in this series and vice versa.

- Book 1: *Zero Sum*
- Book 2: *Zero Day*
- Book 3: *Zero Base*
- Book 4: *Zero Trust*

For more information about Binary Hackers:
JanThompson.com/binary

ABOUT JAN THOMPSON

USA Today bestselling author Jan Thompson writes clean and wholesome contemporary Christian romance with elements of women's fiction, Christian romantic suspense with an air of mystery, and inspirational international thrillers with threads of sweet Christian romance. Jan's books are for readers who love inspiring stories of faith, hope, and love in Jesus Christ.

Raised on a tropical island in the eastern hemisphere, Jan now lives and writes in the western hemisphere. Her international background gives her a unique multicultural and multiracial perspective to her novels and books. The island has never left her, and she reminisces about beach life in her beach romance novels.

When Jan is not busy writing small-town stories, she writes big-city romantic suspense and international technothrillers, a nod to her previous career in computer science. She weaves technology with human interests, reflecting the current and future digital world. And romance. There's always romance.

Beyond the printed page, Jan is a wife, mother, family scribe, avid reader, occasional artist, erstwhile pianist, and chief of staff to the family cat.

Find out more about Jan Thompson:
JanThompson.com

Subscribe to Jan's book news mailing list:
JanThompson.com/newsletter

For God so loved the world
that He gave His only begotten Son,
that whoever believes in Him
should not perish
but have everlasting life.
—John 3:16